The Ballad
of
Pinewood Lake

By Jory Sherman
from Tom Doherty Associates

The Ballad of Pinewood Lake
Grass Kingdom
The Barons of Texas
The Baron Range
The Baron Brand
Horne's Law
The Medicine Horn
Song of the Cheyenne
Trapper's Moon
Winter of the Wolf

The Ballad
of
Pinewood Lake

❧

JORY SHERMAN

A Tom Doherty Associates Book
New York

THE BALLAD OF PINEWOOD LAKE

Copyright © 2001 by Jory Sherman

Design by Heidi Eriksen

A Forge Book
Published by Tom Doherty Associates, LLC
175 Fifth Avenue
New York, NY 10010

www.tor.com

Forge® is a registered trademark of Tom Doherty Associates, LLC.

Library of Congress Cataloging-in-Publication Data

Sherman, Jory.
    The ballad of Pinewood Lake / Jory Sherman. — 1st ed.
        p. cm
    "A Tom Doherty Associates book."
    ISBN 0-312-85774-8 (acid-free paper)
        1. Problem families—Fiction. 2. Women alcoholics—Fiction.
3. Country life—Fiction. 4. Authorship—Fiction. 1. Title.

PS3569.H43 B34 2001
813'.54—dc21

                                                    00-048464

First Edition: February 2001

Printed in the United States of America

0   9   8   7   6   5   4   3   2   1

For Charlotte, with all my love

Climb the mountains and get their
good tidings. Nature's peace will flow
into you as sunshine flows into trees.
The winds will blow their own freshness into you, and the storms their
energy, while cares will drop off like
summer leaves.

—John Muir

Part One

~ The Winter ~

There's a certain slant of light,
on winter afternoons,
that oppresses, like the weight
of cathedral tunes.
—Emily Dickinson
"Nature"

~ *Pinewood Lake* ~

Four hours out from Los Angeles I drove into nothingness.
I was surging up to seven thousand feet above sea level, out of
my element, driving a huge rented truck through a snowstorm
that turned the winding road white, blotting out all the lines,
cutting off the definitions of the terrain like a sheet thrown over
an albino landscape.

The ski white snow coming down fast, a big white shroud
between us and Pinewood Lake, tire chains grinding into the
road, the flakes pouring into the open window like dwarf stars
sucked into one of those black holes of the interminable universe.

Heart trying to get back to pumping up the long white winding road.

Sixty-five dollar chains bought for one day for a rented
U-Haul truck. Up to Pinewood Lake, that snowy day, to a new
home, a new place to live, to write, to find the earth again. Let it
snow, let it snow, let the big tires skid on the slippery curves. This
is the revenge of about a hundred thousand lawns against a flatlander trying to live high on the mountain.

It would be easy to go to sleep on this road like the old
pathfinders who found peace in the cold, the white bed of the sub-
zero winters. I drive in a state of hypnosis, gulled by the falling
snow, heart driving to get me up there where the air is even thin-
ner, but less toxic. In my mind I am spewing out tons of coal-like
objects, freeing my lungs, gearing up my body for the altitude
where breath can sear but not pollute. I am a happy man, so deliri-

~11~

ous on the journey to the sky I don't even care if I drive off the mountain.

I don't leave the road, however. I make it and then have tons of furniture and personal possessions to unload into my new home. Angela is following in the old Cadillac with Colin, our young son, and when she gets there she'll find mattresses and records, manuscripts and chairs, lamps and groceries piled in the empty living room of our new home. She'll also find that tons of snow have fallen on the walkway where we were led by the real estate agent just a month ago as he held out the papers for signing.

The ground we bought is invisible.

Yet it is very precious, even so.

~ Angela Paul ~

I have chosen this name for my wife because she is more pure than the earth will allow her to be.

I have created her out of her own image and it is pleasing to my eye.

She looks across the room at me with a handclasp. I take her in my mind under the night of my smile.

She is Angela and I brought her here to Pinewood Lake for a reason. She is to be my woman.

I am to be her man.

There is nothing that cannot be created out of this relationship. We will have a green garden. We will build a home and an Eden. We will look at pines and fall in love every day. We will raise Colin in this place on the mountain where he can feel the sun and smell the fragrances of these trees. He will fish in the lake and catch trout, bass, and catfish. Angela and I will show him how to cook his catch, taste him as he smiles and speaks his excited onomatopoeia.

Angela and Colin.

I'm glad I met her, married her, brought her to this place. I'm glad we had a son who will live in the mountains.

He is so much like her, she so much like him. All of us so much like each other.

We are a trio of many things: winding roads across the United States crimsoned by Arizona sunsets and west Texas sunrises, treks through Baja looking for lost gold in lizard gullies, sails across blue-green waters with silver spray freezing on our faces, salty, sweet as candy at a carnival.

We are together, at first, and we are incongruous.

The three of us: surreal creatures in an amniotic sea of the cosmos, trying to find each other, trying to find the sea we saw in the lake near our new home. No matter.

The lake will find us, eventually.

I have chosen my wife, her name. Our son has chosen us and we will live in this pine land together.

It is a matter of looking and seeing. It is a matter of finding.

We will find what we have to find here.

We will find many things. Many things will find us. I will find Angela. She will find me.

～ *Widow* ～

Shortly after I first met Angela, she was widowed.
I didn't know the details of her husband's death. He was young. He died while skydiving from an airplane south of Perris over Lake Elsinore.

Angela didn't talk about her husband much. Nor her past, in fact. She had begged him not to go skydiving that day. He had been injured once before, apparently.

"Why did he go, then?" I asked her.

"He wanted to test himself. He was afraid."

"He was afraid of skydiving?"

"He was afraid of a lot of things. He always did them anyway."

"But was he a good sky diver?"

"No. I don't think so. I didn't go with him."

"What happened?" I was trying to get at something that Angela was keeping from me.

"I got a call from one of his friends. I knew what the call was about even before I picked up the phone."

"You did? How?"

"You just know. I did. He wanted to die."

My scalp prickled when she told me this. I could see her husband suiting up, pulling on the chute he packed himself, going up in the plane, jumping out, floating out there thousands of feet above the earth, spread-eagling his arms, face flattened by the wind, eyes burning through goggles. Drinking it all in, a last look at life, the earth. Then . . .

"What happened? Didn't he pull his rip cord?"

"He pulled it. His chute tangled up. I don't want to talk about this anymore, Johnny."

But I was angry.

"He pulled his rip cord, then? All right. He had another chute. Did he pull that one, too?"

Angela nodded, but she was far away. She kept these and other things to herself. All the time. It made her mysterious, but it also made her exasperating to someone who wanted to find out about her, about how she thought.

So, both chutes fouled up.

Something haunted her, then. Did he commit suicide? Was that what bothered her? It bothered me. If he did commit suicide, then why? Why? Angela didn't want to talk. I didn't want to think.

~ Colin ~

Colin belongs here in this place.

He is full of the outdoors; he is sunshine. He sees his first squirrel and smiles all over. The squirrel whisks his tail and looks at the blond little boy, pop-eyed, curious. Colin chases him on wobbly legs, squealing with delight. Angela tries to keep him from falling down. The squirrel scampers up a tree and stops, staring at the child, his tail arched, his claws tapping on the bark.

It is a game between creatures.

Colin is like one of the bright flowers that bloom in our yard, yet he is rootless. There is so much to see in his new world here, now that he can toddle. We explain to him what plants are, and birds, and squirrels. He seems to understand, although he cannot talk yet; cannot tell us what he feels, in words.

Instead, he is like sunlight through the leaves: now here, now there, now gone. He is hard to keep up with because he has so much world to see.

Angela has a shadow across her face. She stands between two pines looking at the father and the son. There is something between us she can't fathom. He is her son, but he is also mine. The bond between Colin and me is almost invisible. We belong here very much. Angela belongs here, too, but she doesn't understand this, just yet.

She looks off toward the lake, which we can't see from our chalet.

I can see the lake in her eyes, though.

Beyond the pines that obscure it, the lake blooms with hot springs that feed it from below. It blazes, with silver and time, like something brought out of an old oaken chest. Boats with faceless people float on its shimmering surface. For a moment, in my mind, everything is motionless, even the sun.

Angela turns back to me and I smile at her.

Through the darkness of her thoughts, she smiles back.

"Colin loves it here," I say.

"I know," says Angela.

"Don't you, too?"

"Yes," she says, and the darkness floods her face again.

I hurt for Colin and Angela, for different reasons. I know Angela loves it here, as she says, but it's some kind of a last stand for her. I don't know why yet, but I know I'm right. She is very unhappy. Colin is chasing after life. Life is chasing after him.

~ The Writings ~

I earn my precarious living as a writer. I wasn't writing what I wanted to before we came here, but was determined to get back to the good writing now that I was out of the so-called rat race.

Actually, it's easier for a writer to make money if he's in one of the big three metropolitan centers: Chicago, Los Angeles, or New York. The competition is fierce anywhere you live, but editors and publishers like to see their scribes in the flesh. Deals can be made at lunch, big advances assured at cocktail parties.

Here, away from the publishing world, I have to write for the small markets in order to support my literary craving. There has been no pressure, but there is also very little money—and that can be pressure.

I write for the hairy-chested magazines, the men's adventure stuff like: "I Fought the Invasion of the Nazi S-Girls While Fleeing Rommell's Tanks," or "30,000 Leeches Sucked My Blood on the Orinoco." These are all supposedly "true" stories, but if any of them are really true, I didn't write them. You use a crisp, pseudo-journalist's style, plenty of action, a dash of sex and you can sell these editors such "true" stories as "I Survived the Shark-Infested Waters of Bali for 149 Days," by Joe Blow as told to Johnny Paul.

They even print a hazy photograph of this fictitious Joe Blow so that the piece looks authentic. The "illo," or illustration, is usually a gory rendition taken from the story, with a caption excerpted from the body copy, like, "I leaped in the air as the giant tarantulas ripped at my flesh."

I am so adept at writing these stories that I can get up at four o'clock in the morning, write two of them by eight o'clock, eat breakfast, give them to Angela to type, and be out on the lake fishing by nine.

This is what has kept me going up in Pinewood Lake. This is what has kept me writing late in the evening: poems, stories, and pieces of novels. Pieces of my heart, pieces of my soul. These literary pieces were things that could not be sold immediately. There was no price tag on them.

There were no buyers, except Angela.

She was to pay dearly for them. And so was I.

~ Our New Home ~

W e had spent a lot of money in moving here. I had sold most of the household furniture down the hill in order to finance our relocation to the mountains.

We got here and wondered if we'd be welcome. Some places are hard to move to: people shun you. It wasn't that way here. The people we met, waitresses, mechanics, bartenders, real estaters, all seemed anxious to have us as neighbors.

They were almost overly friendly. Was there a note of desperation in their voices? Angela and I didn't hear it then, if that was the case. There did seem in retrospect, though, to be a plaintive cry for help behind each cordial welcome. Our own paradise was too newly found, however, for us to read the signals that probably were being sent out.

We were welcomed, and that was enough at that time. We were ecstatic about being here in the pines and by the lake. Who needed money? Who needed anything? Not us. We were king and queen of the mountain; we were omnipotent.

Our kingdom shook ominously, however, from a quake that rumbled from within.

The first night at our new home: an hysterical woman screaming outside.

Angela, shredding to pieces before my eyes.

The night swirled around us as she screamed in her drunkenness. I wanted to kill her then. I hated her for spoiling the night, the first night there. She stood out on the road and announced to the world that she was crazy, that the move had been a great shock to her.

I knew this wasn't so.

She loved it here. She loved it as I did. She had to. The shock of change was just too much for her. That had to be it. Our kingdom had to survive. Our lives had just begun.

I quelled my hatred and coaxed her inside the chalet. We were not settled yet. We had trails to roam, hills to climb, picnics to plan.

Upstairs, a light breeze came through the slightly opened window. Snow fell steadily all night as Angela slept. It had been a long time since I'd seen snow gentle the earth like that. I was drunk, too.

I was drunk on snow, on the kingdom of our new home. I was drunk on earth, with the woman I loved, up high in the mountains.

It was as if I had suddenly emerged from dreamtime and had found the world waiting for me. I had to roam its four corners and name everything I saw and map my course as I sang my song.

~ Rivers of Air ~

After we had been here a week or two, we discovered the wind rivers.

They coursed through our small plot of ground, in chalet windows, like the Feather in spring, the Santa Ana after the thaw, and like all the fast rivers that race when the snows melt and pour down rocky beds to bury themselves in the desert.

One night, just after dusk, Angela and I stood on the back porch listening to these awesome rivers of wind that roared through the pine forest. We began to name them, speculating on their origins, their destinations.

There was a cat wind that meowed through the big oak and skittered down to the lake with a clawing intensity. There was the mouse breeze just before it, a trickle in the pines, dying out before the onslaught of the bigger cat wind. We called these winds, these invisible rivers, Cat and Mouse.

A big wind, from the southeast, ripped at our little weather vane on the porch rail and kept it spinning. It seemed to come from a mountain called Humpback. We called this the Humpback river. It was full of snows and freezes, tumbling down the slopes like an avalanche of ice cream cones. We could taste its strawberry freshness as it came on, its chocolate aftertaste as it hurtled by us.

Another wind came from the west, the sea. It circled over a bigger mountain, Santo Grande, and whipped by the back porch with the scariness of bats emerging from a dark cave by the thousands. We called this the Bat river because we could feel its blackness, its teeth and talons tugging at our clothing.

The porch became rather shaky when these wind rivers were in turmoil. We would feel them and become sexually excited.

After dinner, we went upstairs and opened our windows. We listened to the rivers of air. They seemed tamer up there.

We held each other in mock fear.

We made love like wild creatures in a cataclysm.

The smell of the pines wafted through the open windows. The smell of our lovemaking drifted out into the rivers of wind that coursed through the valley. Contagious. Flowing.

We are sure that a lot of people in Pinewood Lake made love on those same nights.

You could almost taste the romance floating through the pines.

It was in the wind. In the rivers of air that are always running full in the channels of the universe.

~ Snowbound ~

Winter came to us again during the night.

Everything was white and soft in the morning. It was very still and I could hear a lot of silences way back in the woods. It was very reassuring to be alone.

I woke up Angela and brought her downstairs, though she was blurred like some painting of Duchamps. We dressed Colin in his new red snowsuit, took him outside, and showed him his first snow. Grinning with excitement, he held out his hand and caught the snowflakes. They melted as soon as they hit. He opened his mouth and snowflakes flew in, like tiny lace hosts at a Catholic Mass, disappearing before he could taste them.

We wanted to be snowed in. We didn't want to go anywhere or see anyone. We just wanted to enjoy the solitude.

It kept snowing all day and no snowplow came down the road. It was as if we had ordered it that way. It was a good day to read and drink beer, to enjoy the cooking smells. I walked out in the snow a couple of times but I didn't want any footprints to mar the white mounds. I shoveled the walk, though. It made our place look more homey.

Angela kept looking out the picture window. She was very happy.

"Isn't it beautiful?" she asked a dozen times.

"I love it," I said.

"Don't you just wish it could stay like this forever?"

"I'd like a few days of it."

"Oh, no, I would like it to snow like this forever. It makes everything in the world look clean and pure and white like a wedding dress. I just wish the world could always be as pure as this, so white and pure, so beautiful."

We were snowed in for five days.

The plow came once, but the snow kept falling. The berm left by the machine made it impossible to dig out. The snowbanks were dirty and hard. We pulled a sled down the road and shopped for groceries at Ollinger's.

It was fun pulling the sled back home. Colin loved the ride through a quiet world of snowflakes and tingling light. It took us an hour or so, and when we got back we felt like pioneers even though the store was less than a mile from our house.

The woods were motionless. Outside our window, it was different: the squirrels, the jays and juncoes were there gobbling the peanut hearts and birdseed I kept in constant supply. They were our only neighbors that day.

The street was hushed as the snow kept falling.

It was peaceful. I could understand Angela's liking it that way. We didn't have to be anywhere, do anything. We worked. I wrote and she typed my manuscripts. We got more work done than we usually did, with effortless ease.

Yet people can't live in a snow white vacuum. The sun must shine again, the world must be encountered. After five days we watched the sun come out, the snow begin to melt. It was very sad. We felt as though we had lost something.

But maybe we had learned that we could live close together without getting cabin fever. We felt we could have lasted for months in a snowbound world.

We liked the closeness, the silence, the solitude. We felt different, somehow, with the sky so close, ourselves part of the earth's weather.

We had changed, for a brief spell, into other someones. We were not really our old selves. We were new.

We were winter people.

~ The Bears ~

Angela bundled Colin up in his red snowsuit. She and I wore ski jackets, light, comfortable. The snow wasn't very deep and we wanted to go out in the woods to see what the silence was like. We walked across the road and through the pines. The sky was the color of a mourning dove's breast. Our breaths made thin ephemeral clouds as we hiked up the sloping path just barely indented to show its existence. The snow was soft and trackless until we passed.

Above a nearby church camp, vacant in the winter, the pines got thicker and taller. There was a ridge to the east and a glade just before it, open, with still bigger trees. Some fallen logs lay strewn over the snowy floor. Colin was very quiet, like we. There was nothing to say. It was too solemn, too beautiful to spoil with words.

We climbed over a deadfall. My heart quickened. There, in the snow, still fresh, were the tracks of three bears. The tracks were unmistakable. One set of prints was large, another medium-size. Still another set was small. A cub and its parents, I thought. My blood tingled in my veins.

"Bear," I told Angela.

"Where?"

"Somewhere nearby."

I looked around, but saw nothing. The tracks went down another path, one that went through the church camp. They were still steaming.

"They're going down to raid the garbage cans at the camp," I told her.

"We'd better get out of here. I'm afraid of bears. They're so mean and ugly. They look like mean rich people in fur coats and they have big teeth and claws. Let's get away, please, please let's get away quick."

"Yes, we should," I said. My blood was chuting through a millrace.

We could hear the bears a few moments later. They were grunting and laughing down by the camp buildings. I remembered it was Sunday. We saw them then, three black bears, toddling around the church, like a little family. They looked almost human, like roly-poly people in thick fur coats. We angled away from them toward our home. I was glad we were upwind of them. The bears don't hibernate up here. They get hungry during the winter and come down to the cabins looking for food.

I didn't realize until we got back home that Angela had been afraid—more afraid than I was. She was shaking. I asked her why.

"They—they seemed so ominous," she said.

"I thought they were cute."

"If they had seen us, they might have killed us. I wouldn't want to die like that, be clawed and bitten and chewed up into pieces." She shivered with the thought. "Yes, I think the bears would have killed us all."

"I doubt it. They would have run off, probably."

"They were so big," she said. "I don't like big things like that. Big things scare me. They were just big and mean."

"All but the little one."

"That's why they would have killed us. Because of the cub."

"Well, we're safe now, Angela. Nothing happened."

"No," she said solemnly, "nothing happened. But I'm still scared. I'm scared to death."

She was still trembling long after we had dropped the conversation. Something had happened to Angela. I don't think she felt very much at home so close to the woods. I think that's when she first set out, subconsciously perhaps, to destroy herself—and began, too, to destroy me.

~ Dawn ~

Dawn was about her like a shroud.

I had made love to Angela a half hour ago. Now she was unconscious again while the morning startled our windows with a hundred colors, a thousand sounds, a million impressions. I felt fine, alert, because Angela had also made love to me. That is the good thing about her. She is very feminine, very sure about that important part of herself. She is receptive, but she is also dynamic, not uncertain about her ability to give love.

In sleep, though, she is like a woman beneath a sea, a lake.

Her hair floats on the pillow, her mouth opens soundlessly, her neck moves with the struggle to articulate her dreams. I watch her like a man torn between knowledge and fear of the unknown, an Adam on the brink of discovery. She has something to say. I am not sure I want to hear it. What she says might come from the subconscious, what she sees might disturb my complacency here at Pinewood Lake.

She is like Cleopatra, lying in state.

Dawn about her like a shroud.

Yet she is alive, saying something. I love her.

I am listening for her breath, watching her closed eyes.

I am looking deep into the snowfall outside our dawn window. And I am trying to understand Angela.

In her deep dream sleep, she is perhaps trying to understand me.

~ A View of the Lake ~

The first time I saw the lake was at night.

It danced like a tilting mirror under the phosphorous lamp of the moon.

I was standing on the shore near a lone pine tree looking into its depths, across its waters dancing like a cloudy mirror, showing me the moon on a bright ribbon of highway across its middle. Dancing like a siren of space, showing me its captured planets wavering in icy fall waters. Dancing like an ocean with vast expanses, stretching to all the shores of earth with the lights of the town and the heavens caught in its waters, with the fishes of the world moving long and silver in its silent tides. The lake, dancing, dancing in my wondering eyes, a great ocean of time and spatial enigmas, dancing like a shimmering wheat field when the winds come whispering across the plains.

I'm glad I saw the lake at night that first time.

I wasn't really ready for it, although I saw a lot of things in its mirror.

I saw the town and the mountains reflected along its shores, turned upside down for study by some nocturnal scientist. I saw the lamps of fishes arcing through the night like silver blades. I saw their green shapes take form close to shore as they wandered like shadows painted for Halloween. I saw the lost shapes of Indians in the clouds reflected in the silent shore waters, heard their keening for the lost land. I saw, as I moved closer to the lake, my own reflection, torn by the night, the dark refractions veined by the moon.

The moving fishes know my heart and the way I hum a song.

This lake is my birthing place and my ultimate grave. It's my mother and the dark father who comes to row me across its deeps. I know this as surely as I stand at its shore.

No matter, we all have this ticking thing in our breasts. Like the moon, like the dark skies that visit every day's night. A shawl we ignore or wrap close around our throats.

I put my hand into the lake's waters. A trout strikes twenty feet away. We are brothers. He remembers the pyramids, swimming on dry sandy land; I remember a land of sky blue waters and the physician's hand, all of us moving toward something we came from a long time of stars ago.

I leave the lake, thinking.

At home, I take off my coat, open the refrigerator. There, frozen, is the lake again. I drink it from my tap and go to bed. I dream of dancing mirrors, of ices and moons.

~ *The Bars of Pinewood Lake* ~

We came here to live the simple life, but already realize that it's complicated here, too. The community is small, compressed, with too many bars per capita. The bars keep the sad and angry people off the streets. They spill out at two A.M., these sad and angry people, to go home in a stupor, leaving some of their sadness and angriness in the Kaos down on Main Street, Pluto's a few doors away, and Archers still farther down where Main meets Lake Street. The Vega Inn, where Lake rejoins Main Street in a T shape, is where the tourists stay and where the higher class locals go for "attitude adjustment." Out Main, there's Big Ossie's, and farther out in Pine City there is the Sticks, a beer bar owned by Bud Karon. There is a sign in the Sticks saying, "Hangovers installed and serviced." Everyone thinks that sign's a riot.

The Kaos and Archers open real early in the morning. People with their hands shaking come in there to get well, but really get sicker. The Kaos is where the motorcyclists come to drink. They park their raked choppers out front and swagger inside on weekends to put down the citizens. That's where they would pick up girls if there were any girls in there to pick up. The girls are all at Pluto's or Big Ossie's. Big Ossie has two girls living upstairs over the bar who serve as the only two prostitutes in Pinewood Lake. They get a lot of action, I guess.

We do not go to the bars very often anymore. They were interesting when we first came here, but now that Angela realizes where the poison is, we do not like to tempt fate. The band at the

Kaos was nice to listen to once, but we are tired of hearing the same songs over and over, of seeing the same people every weekend. Even the new people look like the old ones.

It has taken us a while to realize that the simple life is only at home. Some people can't function on simplicity. It drives them nuts. It drives them to the bars.

Angela, I think, could have thrived on simple things, if she hadn't made them complex through her drinking.

That's what caused her addiction, perhaps.

The people who go to the bars are sure glad they're not alcoholics. They can hold their drinks, they say.

Angela pitied them. Seeing their hands shake made her fearful. That's why she didn't drink in the bars, only at home, where things were simpler, less complex. I've seen her spoil simplicity several times here. She spoiled it with straight swallows of poison. I have wept to see her personality split in two after consuming several drinks. I have seen her drown before my very eyes. I have seen her far off, in a chair, looking as though she were inside a lake she had created with her own tears, her voice muffled in the waters, her hair straggled like weeds growing from the bottom, her eyes pouring out more sadness and anger than our small world could stand.

~ *Wounded* ~

I was chopping kindling for the fire when my axe slipped, wounding me.

Pain surged through my shin; my shadow on the snow went away for a moment. Lights spun around in my head. I wanted to kick the stump, hurl the axe through the trees. Tears stung my eyes.

My shadow came back to my body.

I yelled.

Angela came running out the back door. She thought I was just yelling like I always do. About nothing.

"Are you all right, Johnny?" she asked.

I glared at her in pain. My leg felt numb and wet and amputated.

"No," I said through clenched teeth. "I'm not all right. I've just severed my leg. Take me to a doctor. Take me to the morgue."

She ran down the porch stairs, still uncomprehending. I hated her.

"Are you okay?" she asked again. As if she were mindless, blind.

I was certain she was an idiot. My leg was either gone or swollen to the size of the oak next to where I had been standing.

I called her eighty-five different names, some biblical, some better known in the earthy books I'd written, some completely original. The bitter words bounced off of her like marshmallows. Angela knew me well enough.

She saw the blood, the torn cloth of the jeans next to my shin. She was very calm as I passed out, falling conveniently into her arms.

"Poor Johnny," she said when I woke up, on the couch, my trousers off, my wound bandaged. Angela and Colin were there like ministering angels.

"Minestrone angels," I said mysteriously.

"What?" she asked.

"I'd like some soup. And thanks."

Angela kissed me. She thought I was delirious. And maybe I was. Colin kept saying, "Daddy," and I took him onto my chest. He had a bottle in his hand and looked like an orphan. Beautiful.

"You gave yourself a good whack," Angela said, rattling the cupboards. I was annoyed by noises and she knew that, too. I think she wanted me to come back to life, to yell. "I fixed it up, though. It wasn't as deep as it looked." She sounded disappointed.

Damn, she was sweet. She fed me soup, while Colin sat next to his wounded father, understanding somehow what I wanted him to understand. I was the consummate actor.

"It wasn't as deep as it looked," Angela said again. "I thought there would be a lot more blood. I thought I would see all of your muscles and ligaments all torn up and bloody, the bone sticking out. I thought I might have to call someone to cut off your leg." She seemed lost in a state of mind that I couldn't fathom. She had a dreamy look in her eyes that almost made me shudder.

"No," I said, sipping my soup. "But you're deeper than you look."

She had done an expert job of dressing my slight wound. This wasn't training. This was love.

"I finished the kindling while you were asleep," she said. "Colin helped me. I liked chopping the wood. I pretended each log was someone who had hurt you and I was killing it, smashing it, cutting legs off."

She spoke of the wood chopping with a strange passion.

I looked at both of them, at the fireplace. There was the wood. A couple of the pieces were bloody.

"Nestle to me," I said.

She and Colin made me feel like a bed of strawberries being tucked in for the winter.

After a while she started a fire while I lay on the couch like a medaled soldier with his sexy nurse. I wished I had a bandage around my forehead, a patch over one eye, shrapnel in my leg. I didn't feel any pain from the axe wound.

"Does it hurt much?" she asked when the fire was blazing.

"Umm," I said.

"I know it must," she said. "I'll put some more salve on it when we go to bed. Do you want some aspirin?"

"No, sweetheart. I'll tough it out."

Humphrey Bogart perfectly. John Wayne at the river. Johnny Paul in love with his wife.

It felt very fine to be wounded that night. The fire was warm and so was Angela. So was I, even though I was almost an amputee.

The next day I sharpened the axe and Angela chopped kindling like a pro while I watched her, a Civil War veteran who had been to town with a beautiful lady, spent the night in her soft silk bed, drunk on her perfume.

~ *Marianne* ~

In a moment of leaves, during autumn, she appears suddenly, out of a swirling wind that blinds the eyes, makes you wonder about the fate that hums like electricity in odd places. You don't expect her. One moment she isn't there, the next she is. Dark hair, too-red lips, eyes off center like a painting by Modigliani, legs that seem too spindly to carry her proud hips, coat wrapped about her like a shield against the slings and arrows of the world.

This is Marianne, a composite of many women, here and everywhere.

She gingerly steps out into the chill, unfeeling, like some beautiful soulless zombie, staring into a somber void, walking careful as though picking her way barefooted through the cherry fires in the hearts of coals. She is trying to appear steady, sober, but her mind is back there in the bar, in the empty glass, lost somewhere there in the cold dregs of ice melting at the bottom in a pale amber pool. A quick drink at dusk; then two, three, then this: making her way to her battered Ford, fumbling with numb hands for the keys.

This is Marianne, an alcoholic, helpless against herself, against the day, the night, helpless before everything.

She finds her car, opens the door, and lurches inside.

The ignition key finds its way into the wavering dash.

She sits back in her seat and tries to focus beyond the steering wheel. She hums disconsolately a song she heard somewhere in the background on a gaudy jukebox, but can't find the right pitch, her tone off-key like the wind that sometimes gets lost in the autumn mountains.

Marianne riffles through her purse, a big purse, fat from carrying secret bottles of vodka, brandy, ponies of wine, finds the package of breath mints. Works one loose, carries it to her mouth, worries it around with her tongue. She feels better somehow when the taste seems to blot out the other taste: dry rain-soaked wood, bitter as green acorns. She sighs and turns the ignition key. The car coughs into life. She focuses on a mist outside the car, tosses a look behind her, puts the gearshift into reverse, and backs out into the darkening street.

She drives home, somehow, through the blurred streets, up the blurred land, and into the blurred driveway. The breath mint gives her confidence and she gets out of her car. She composes herself with a fleeting sober thought, gathers herself together like a phoenix rising out of casket ashes, walks up to her door, and lets herself inside, pasting a wan smile on her face like an aged actress called once more before the footlights.

The baby is crying. His face is dirty, his diapers are soggy and full of excrement. He is Tad, on the floor, alone. Little Jill is in the kitchen, seven years old, trying to open a can of beans. Rick, three, is playing with a wire at the table, oblivious to Tad's screams in the next room. Marianne's husband, Bill, is not home from work yet. He's down the hill having one last snort with the boys, knowing he must delay his homecoming as long as possible. He is finding he can't face it either.

This isn't all there is to it, of course.

Marianne has tried to commit suicide at least fourteen times. She has been dried out, jailed, sobered up, talked to, condemned, beaten, you name it. She has tried Alcoholics Anonymous, after being committed three times in the last year to a mental ward. She has tried, but she has slipped off. She has tried to cut down, with beer, wine, watered-down gin. Nothing has worked. Her system both craves and rejects alcohol.

Yet she continues to have these nightmare episodes, full of hazy leaves and uncertain winds, snatches of songs heard in cave-like dens where her craving takes her. She sometimes takes up with other men. She doesn't know their faces, sometimes knows their names. She moves in and out of her homebody existence like a wraith, sometimes alive, sometimes in a kind of limbo that mocks her consciousness, twists things around, blanks out whole chunks of her life, makes disaster out of the others.

She is scarred. Mentally and physically. Her family watches her die, helpless to come to her side and snatch her up from the terrible sucking whirlpool that seems to be taking her down, down, down like a straw with dark hair and red lips and spindly legs. Her children are alone, her husband too horrified to try anymore. Alcohol has beaten him, too, and he will either go away, bewildered, or stay and go with her into the sodden days of wine and roses.

Marianne has tried, but now something else has come up. Years of drinking, years of not eating, her liver taking the brunt of this assault, have taken their toll. Her body is breaking down, ravaged by the onslaught of her ambivalent affair with the bottle. Infection sets in, organs collapse, her skin aches in every pore after each drunken episode that she can't remember.

She called me one night after weeks of antibiotics and a slip or two on wine and beer. She said she was going to the hospital. Maybe never to return. The doctor had given her his ultimatum: now or never, stop drinking or die, operation or oblivion. She was going; she assured me of this. He was going to open her up like some wounded flower and take out things that once worked well. He was going to cut and sew and patch the broken stems. He was going to pray and hope.

So was I.

Marianne might not come back from this sober journey down the long sad hill, I thought. Her children, Tad, Rick, and Jill, might cry for a long time. Bill might wonder why something like alcoholism struck such a beautiful young woman, his wife. He might wonder why she was unable to survive that last battle with an insidious enemy that he couldn't understand, that few people can conquer with any degree of confidence. He might wonder why she may never reach another birthday, never vote again, never make the home he wanted.

Marianne will wonder, too, whether she lives or dies, why she had this disease so young. She was only twenty-three years old. An alcoholic. A child. A statistic. A tragedy.

Marianne of Pinewood Lake, of the world.

Was she a young shadow of Angela? When I thought of this terrible lost girl, I became afraid of the past, Angela's past, frightened of the future.

~ Angela's Past ~

When you love someone very much it doesn't matter who he or she is, where that person comes from.

At first. Then, it seems, you want to find out more about the individual. You miss knowing that person when he, or she, was a child. You miss all those years before you met.

Angela was an enigma to me, even though I fell in love with her from the first moment I saw her. She had a poise that impressed me. She was quietly beautiful, without guile, ostentation. She was interested in me.

I never spoke to her until after her husband's death. We met by chance at a coffee shop one morning. She was a woman I had admired from a distance, loved unrequitedly. Sometimes an unrequited love is the best of all. It cannot be spoiled by anything much.

Angela seemed glad to see me, to talk to me. We drank two cups of coffee apiece. She was silent only about herself, about her past. She was going to college then. She had to have a career now that her husband was gone. He had fallen out of the sky one day and left her all alone.

Later, after we knew each other better, I told her I loved her. Her relatives, whom I had never met, thought it was all right to get married again. So Angela said. I gathered that friends of her and her husband were unhappy about it. A year wasn't a long enough mourning time. For them. Angela never came right out and said it, but I gathered they were vicious to her. That could account for her reticence to expose too much of herself. Or her past.

I got the feeling, more than once, that Angela turned part of herself away from me. Her face, for instance, was seldom revealed to me except when she was asleep. She was always blurred in photographs. Or, at night, when I would look across the room at her, part of her face would be in shadow.

She and her husband, I learned, went to a lot of parties. There was a lot of drinking. After the funeral, there was a big party at Angela's, the widow's home.

After we were married, I seldom saw her drink, however. Yet I knew she was drinking. I'd find glasses half-filled with vodka or whiskey hidden in the linen closet or underneath the kitchen sink. Her face would be blurred sometimes in reality.

When you love someone very much, you don't see very much.

Angela, and her past, were opaque.

Sometimes she would catch me looking at her.

"Don't look at me," she would say.

But I would sneak another peek at her when she wasn't watching me. In repose, she looked like a woman wearing the shawl of mourning and in her face the sadness of Spanish women saying their beads on *el dia de los muertos*. Prayers for the dead, for all the lost souls gone to eternal light.

~ Radio Station ~

The radio station stays on the air on stormy nights. Even though it's a small station and supposed to sign off at dusk, it is empowered by the FCC to broadcast later during emergencies. The station in Pinewood Lake is KPLK and is practically a one-man operation.

Duke Johnson owns and operates it. He's an electronic genius, but can't speak the English language well. He's country, though, and the locals enjoy listening to him murder the commercials they've paid good money to get on the air. Any word that has more than two syllables is sure to be butchered by Duke. He is at his best giving the news.

In all the time I've listened to him, he's never pronounced a foreign name or country correctly. His announcers are not much better. In fact, I think he hires them because they are not really top disc jockeys. He hates sharpies, yet he's one of the shrewdest men in Pinewood Lake.

Duke was on the air one night when the snows blocked all the roads. He played country-western music in between the bobbling of announcements.

"Well," he said, "it's still snowing over here at KPLK and we want to give you a word from Jenny's Liquors and Delicatessen. They've got some great stuff down there: meats and liquors of any kind you fancy. Jenny is always on hand to help you make your selections. Right on the boulevard in Pinewood, make your next stop at Lenny's Jiquors, er, ah, Jenny's Liquors. They're the best."

Then he went on to say that chains were required on all roads and the temperature was 28 degrees above zero, with the barometer down around 29.2 millibars. Then he talked about his dog, Taco, out bouncing around in the snow. He talked about the terrible work the snowplows were doing and how they always leave his street till last. He said, "If I didn't have a Jeep, I'd never be able to get to the radio station."

He talked about this injustice for fifteen minutes and then told about his plans to have an FM station. He said several local groups had thwarted his efforts in that direction, including the FCC, the Forest Service, the cable TV company, and fifteen merchants whom he wouldn't mention. He forgot all about the snow, the emergency broadcasts.

Later on, he garbled a new weather forecast and signed off. He put on a patriotic record and then tinkered around the station until midnight, completely happy.

He drove home through the heavy drifts, his mind full of wires and tubes, circuits and strange unintelligible words. The red lights on his radio towers cast an eerie glow over the snow.

He is the heartbeat of Pinewood Lake, the voice of its many people, though he feels he is a loner. When he signs off the air, it is always very still and empty over the lake.

As if the gods had departed and left only their inscrutable beacons pulsing in the night, voiceless as the pyramids and ziggurats built by the Anunaki thousands of years ago.

~ The Villagers ~

Everyone in the village seemed shadowy those winter days. We would see them at the post office, in the market, at the bars, the movie, but we didn't really know them. They drifted in and out of places like strangers. They were comfortable in their surroundings but they didn't really see us as friends. Perhaps we were shadows to them.

It is not that they weren't friendly. They were, superficially, at least. They all seemed to have been here a long time. We were newcomers. We had the feeling we'd be newcomers for many years. They gave us that impression.

The established people were the strangers, really. We were friends with the artists, Kathy and Tommy, and with the Goldmans. Peter Goldman was not very friendly. He was a social climber, wanted to be with the village establishment. Lorraine, his wife, seemed to be on the fence. She liked to be with the artists, but she had to climb up the chicken coop walls with her husband.

We met a big friendly fellow who lived in Pine City. He was Art DeLand and he raised worms for a living. His wife, Holly, was a wino, but they were both nice people. When they got drunk they turned nasty, but it took a lot to get them drunk. They were not part of the village establishment.

The friendliest people, but the most dangerous, were the barflies. These were the old-timers who had long since lost hope for anything. Some of them had come here to open a business.

When that failed they started drinking with the other losers at the Kaos, Pluto's, Big Ossie's, or the Sticks. In fact, Art used to own the Sticks out in Pine City. He was on the fringe of the barfly group, on his way down to join them if his worm ranch ever failed. Most of the people in the bars were bartenders or cocktail waitresses, or fry cooks or janitors. Some of them had never been anything.

On the upper level were the dentists, the real estate people, the merchants, the doctors, the veterinarians. They tried to associate with some of the lower castes on Sunday nights but it never worked. The barflies knew the dentists and merchants were slumming.

It was really hard to find your own level in Pinewood Lake. The levels kept changing and you really didn't know which group was compatible with your philosophy. I became a chameleon, a drifter. I was friendly to all, intimate with none. This got me branded as a loner, I suppose, because we very seldom got invited anywhere. Maybe that's what Angela couldn't stand. Maybe she could read this society subconsciously. It was an odd society.

Full of strangers, full of shadows.

~ *Thinking* ~

Out in the snow, Angela stood there like a statue, flakes whirling around her. Colin was still asleep. It was early morning and I had been writing in my room. Angela couldn't see me as I looked at her through the large picture window. She held a cup of coffee in her hand, its steam melting the flakes that came near it. I was glad I had bought her those warm furry boots, the blue ski jacket.

"What're you thinking about?" I asked her when I walked outside, wearing a Levi's jacket, sniffing the wetness of the pleasant little snowstorm.

She turned with red cheeks, a bright smile.

"Umm, it feels good," she said. "I was just thinking how lucky we are to live here."

"Yeah. I've been up for hours."

"I know. I wish I had."

She was very happy. The snow specked her dark hair, lined her eyelashes with faint chalk lines.

"Do you want to go sledding?" I asked. "We could take Colin."

"No," she said. "I just want to drink it all in. He's still asleep."

"Deep asleep, huh?"

"He almost looks like he's dead," she said, and I felt a chill ripple up my spine as if someone had injected me with a transfusion of ice water. But there was not a trace of guile on her face. I shrugged her comment off as just another of her peculiar similes.

She walked out into the lane where the snow was swirling down furiously. Where she had first stood, the pines had sheltered her. Now her hair began to whiten. I followed her to the edge of the road.

She looked up in the sky and blinked her eyes. She stuck out her tongue and tasted the snow. I was glad she was there. Angela seldom got up this early.

For a minute, she looked like a child.

I just watched her, trying to listen for her thoughts. She didn't say anything. She just looked around, up and down the lane, out into the forest. You could see only a few trees dusted with flour-like snow blowings. They seemed ghostly in the stillness of the early morning.

As I watched, the snow covered her dark hair and clung. When she turned to me, finally, from wherever she had been, she looked old, gray-haired. I was startled, unprepared.

"Do you love me?" she asked, an undertone of desperation in her voice.

"I love you," I said, slightly shocked at the question. "I'll always love you."

She grayed there, looking at me with deep dark eyes, aged a hundred years. The snow seemed to want to capture her there in that position for an eternity.

"I'll always love you, too," she said, her voice coming from very far away, from a snowy kiosk building about her like a white tomb. "No matter what you do to me. No matter what happens to us."

I had chills all over my body.

It seemed as if I had been looking into the future, as if a small window had opened in the fabric of time, then closed again very quickly, like the shutter on a camera lens.

~ *Small Towns* ~

Angela didn't like to go anywhere in Pinewood Lake by herself.

She had almost a phobia about it.

When she did go into the village alone, she was always in disguise. At least no one could recognize her. I saw someone who resembled her one day, walking along Pine Knot Boulevard. I crossed the street.

It was Angela, all bundled up. She was carrying a brown sack folded up in her arms.

"I've been to the store," she said. "But nobody saw me, so I was perfectly safe. I felt invisible."

"Why didn't you ride with me?"

"I didn't want to bother you. You were in that place you go to all the time. Where I can't ever go."

I knew she was talking about those times when I was thinking of a scene or a story. That always bothered her. But I didn't know she thought that I was really gone, just because I was silent and looking inward instead of outward. But I had really been gone this day. I had been gone a long time. I hadn't known she wanted to go into town. Our home was within walking distance, but we usually rode together in the car.

"I'll take you home," I said.

The sack clinked when she got into the car.

"Where's Colin?" I wanted to know.

"Asleep. Dead to the world. I was gone only a minute."

Anger wrenched my mind out of its socket.

"You left Colin by himself? What the hell's the matter with you?"

Anger turned Angela to silence. Always.

I raced home, swerving madly on the corners. Colin was awake, crying. I grabbed him up in my arms and held him close. Angela was waiting for us when we came downstairs. The sack had disappeared. Her eyes glittered. She appeared calm.

"Colin was scared," I said. "He thought we'd deserted him."

Nothing.

"Don't you have anything to say? What the hell was in that sack? Booze?"

"This town is so small you can't do anything here without everyone knowing about it." She seemed to be talking to herself. I stared at her in disbelief. "Small towns get you," she continued. "They always do. They crush you. They eat you up. They make you do things you hate yourself for for the rest of your life."

I didn't realize Angela had come from a small town.

"You're drunk!" I shouted.

But she was deaf and no longer heard me, off in that world of hers where it was dark and narrow and demons danced in the dim light of smoldering fires. A place that Dante knew, where all who entered must abandon all hope.

~ *Worms* ~

Art DeLand had big plans for his worms in the spring.
"I'll make a fortune," he said. "I've got worms coming in from Florida, from Texas, from Riverside. Red worms and night crawlers. I'm going to have the biggest ranch in the mountains."

Art is a big fellow of French descent. He is always scheming. The worms were his latest brainstorm. Before that, he had owned the Sticks out in Pine City and had been involved, I gather, with the law. "Everybody steals," he said to me one day, "and that's the secret of success."

He had been fired from his last job as bartender. He was making change out of his pocket. Got caught.

"I'm going to call my place the King Worm Ranch," he told me, "after that big ranch in Texas. My worms will be bigger, redder, meaner, longer living, livelier than any worms on the hill."

At that time the sporting goods stores, during the summer, bought their worms from down the hill.

"They're reliable," one merchant told me. "Hell, we've had twenty guys up here try to raise worms. They couldn't deliver. We need worms for the tourists who come up here."

Art was going to change all that.

"Come on out," he said, "and see my ranch."

On a clear day, Angela, Colin, and I drove out in my weakening Cadillac to see Art and his wife. He showed me the "ranch." In a shed out back. He had built bins that looked like pinewood coffins, filled them with manure and heating elements, hung light bulbs over each, got him a small garden pitchfork, cartons of worm containers, labels, charts, brochures, and even some rabbits and chinchillas to produce manure.

"This is the King Worm Ranch," he announced proudly, a glass of nearly straight Scotch in his hand. His wife, Holly, was half-crocked on wine, smiling at me like a cut-open watermelon.

"Any worms yet?" I asked.

He grinned like William Buckley Jr., like one of his buck rabbits. He took the small pitchfork and turned some manure. Worms scriggled everywhere in the upturned crap. "There they are," he said. "See the little ones, the thin white stuff. Those are babies."

I saw them.

"They'll number in the millions by spring," he said.

"No kidding?"

"I got fifty thousand from Texas, another twenty thousand from Florida. Look over here at the night crawlers."

We went to a heated bin and he turned a clump of manure over. I saw a bunch of dead worms, big, grotesque things that were already desiccating, shriveling up like worm mummies. Art looked very sad.

"Well, some of them died on the way here," he explained. He kept turning over the clumps of dark compost but I never saw a living night crawler. "The temperature's at an even seventy degrees," he said.

"Maybe they're too cold," I said. It was about 34 degrees outside and about 28 degrees inside the shed, or less.

"Naw, it's warm enough. The trip shook them up."

I asked Art how he could possibly earn a living up here from worms.

"It's easy," he said. "They sell for seventy-five cents a box retail. Fifty worms in each. I'll have millions by spring. Of course, we have to worry about stampedes."

"Stampedes?"

"If there's lightning or noise, the worms stampede. It's a hell of a mess. They crawl over their bins and up the walls and everywhere. You have to catch them and sing to them.

"Sing to them?"

"Yeah. They're like cattle. That's why I call this the King Worm Ranch."

Holly was completely obliterated when we went back into the house. Angela was playing with Colin, sipping on a glass of wine, sociably.

"Let's go, honey," I said. She and Colin came with me. We said good-bye to Art, who waved and smiled from the doorway. Holly couldn't make it to the door. There was a sign outside proclaiming the King Worm Ranch.

As we drove away, I thought I heard his worms lowing in the distance, like whiteface cattle being bedded down for the night. I thought I heard Art singing a cowboy song to his worms. Tomorrow, I thought, he'll heat the branding irons and get to work. He'll round up the strays in the south forty and bring them into the corral. He'll be all right. He'll make it to market along the Chisholm Trail.

If those damned worms didn't stampede. Art would make it all right. Those ranchers know what they're doing.

~ *Look at Us* ~

I sat at a bar one afternoon and watched the town coagulate.

It was after working hard on a poem and disagreeing with my wife. I should have gone skiing. I should have hiked through the woods.

Instead, I had a beer at Big Ossie's.

Miriam was fighting with her alcoholic husband. Her hair was straggly. Her eyes hurt you when you looked at them. Her breasts were better left alone.

She must have been a beautiful woman, once.

Harry was out of work.

His eyes were quite bleary. He looked old and tired. I tried not to look at the veins that made purple maps of the Napa Valley on his nose and cheeks. His face looked like a blurred aerial view of the wine country up there. I felt sorry for him.

Belinda was waiting to go to work at the biggest nightclub in town. She had about four hours to wait and she was drinking a tall Scotch and soda. She looked healthy. Big girl, blond hair, big legs, nice breasts, a Valkyrian harshness about her young puffy face.

"I've seen the maps of Piri Reis," I thought she said.

Of course she said nothing like this at all.

Her voice was as blurred as her face in the mirror behind the bar.

Bud, the bartender, was trying to keep up with it all. This was his eighteenth job in Pinewood Lake. He had been divorced six times. He was very thin and handsome. He had a nice smile.

He knew how to mix good drinks, make pleasant conversation. He looked tired, disconsolate.

"Look at us," he said later. "We're all drunk."

"Yes," I agreed.

"I don't drink, Johnny," he told me. "But I've been on a dry drunk for a long time. Hell, just look at us. All of us."

I looked at all of us, at the desert and the mountains, and I saw what he meant. We might have been sitting at a tavern in the Tigris and Euphrates valley more than ten thousand years ago, watching the last Anunaki taking off in the last space shuttle, the cabin crammed with disillusioned Nephilim.

We were all very thirsty for very different reasons.

We were all very drunk.

~ The Old Cadillac ~

The old Cadillac was deteriorating more each day.

Why do people hang on to things like that? The snob in me had been dying ever since we came to Pinewood Lake. The Caddie, with personalized plates, was rusting, coughing, overheating, puffing from the altitude. It was like an albatross around my neck. The seats of leather were cracking, the seams showing the stuffing underneath as they opened up like wounds in a dying animal.

Yet we couldn't get rid of it. It was our only transportation.

What about walking?

We like to walk. Carrying is another matter. Why not get a wagon? we wondered. Hell, every time we thought about getting a wagon, we got in the Caddie and drove where we wanted to go.

It was dumb.

This was our past, our old dreams of glory sitting out in front of the house like a tombstone.

Sometimes I wanted to just let it sit there and die. Or I wanted to call someone and have it carted away. But we'd spent nearly two thousand dollars on it in the last year or so. Just to keep it running.

Stupid.

I realized something important one day when Angela and I were driving the car back from the repair shop. It hit me obliquely, like when a fighting bull finally realizes that the cape is not the enemy anymore.

The Cadillac didn't belong in our world. It was part of nine-to-five, punching time clocks, impressing the neighbors, driving through Beverly Hills.

We weren't that way anymore.

We didn't need this doubtful status.

Still, we held on to the old car, afraid to break all ties, all umbilicals to the money world of Los Angeles.

I began to think that not only was the car financially fatal, but morally fatal as well. The more I held on to it, the more I was hooked into a world where I didn't belong.

My morals are terrible, apparently.

My finances were not much better.

The Cadillac stayed on with us for a long time. We were all dying together.

~ *Evening* ~

Good music and a fire, night around us in the chalet, its air
pouring through the open window after dusk. Umm, I felt
content. The coolness was necessary. We needed the fire to make
us feel as cozy as we wanted to after most of the snow had melted.

Our windows were undraped, and the pines in our yard all
seemed to get closer to the house. Angela was on the couch with
me that night. Colin was asleep upstairs, breathing the fragrances
of the evening. His cheeks were rosy from being outside all day,
from being alive.

The fire crackled through our thoughts. We had wood left
from the winter storms, pine and piñon, burning excitingly in the
chimney's shadowy cave. We had had a good meal of beef bour-
guignonne and rice, wine, after-dinner B & Bs like rich people.

We were rich. The writing was done for the day, the boots
off, the fire lit, the living room nestling us with a kind of furry
comfort.

"We should do something tomorrow," I said to Angela, who
was staring into the fireplace.

"What do you want to do?"

"Go up to the gold valley. Picnic."

"I can make sandwiches."

"If the roads are open, we should go up there."

"It's so nice here," she said. "I don't really want to go out."

"Do you really love it?"

"Of course." There was no feeling in her voice. She sounded as if she were reciting a line from a play that didn't mean anything to her.

Was I pushing too hard? I guess I wanted her to see our home here through my eyes. I lived in the mountains once, in Colorado, and this is my Colorado again, only I am the father, not the child.

I thought of Colin, asleep upstairs. Innocent. He would have this heritage. Someday.

Angela didn't understand the referents. I pouted. Maybe she did. But did she? I didn't want to question her too much. What if she didn't like it? Would I have moved back down the mountain?

I felt a dryness in my throat. I wanted to be reassured, but I wasn't going to press it. She liked it here. Surely she did. I wanted to make sure she had a good life, one free of problems. It was a big order.

The log popped like an explosive shot. We jumped and laughed at our fright.

No need for worry. It was a good night and we were together.

Nothing could go wrong. Not in this fine place.

~ *Before a Storm* ~

A jingle of leaves. A catch in the throat. A vagrant breeze out of nowhere, riffling underfoot. Something.

I couldn't put my finger on it.

I looked at Colin and felt an ache in my throat.

My dear son, I love him so.

Angela, nearby, sensed my discomfort in that lull before the odd storm.

There was no snow on the ground. Autumn had come again in the middle of winter. We looked up at gathering clouds, gray things, a flotilla of lumbering leviathans on their own surreal sea.

"What's the matter, Johnny?"

"Nothing."

"You're so tense. You make me nervous inside. I feel like you're going to explode at any minute and murder us."

"I am not tense, Angela."

Yet I was tense. There was some winter still there on the high slopes that bothered me. It was like a baited breath, a prophecy.

"What do you mean, 'murder you'?" I asked.

"I've read about husbands who suddenly murder their wives and children and bury them somewhere. In the lake or in the basement or out in the woods."

"That's crazy. I would never do such a thing."

"It happens all the time, Johnny. People murder their children, their husbands, their wives. When you're tense, you make me feel like I'm going to be murdered."

"I couldn't hurt you. Or Colin."

Colin looked at us. We listened to the building wind. The air was stretched thin and taut, almost crackling with a hidden current of tension.

"Colin, come to Daddy." I lifted him up in my arms and held him close.

He listened to me whisper into his ear.

"Daddy loves you, Colin."

He didn't know the words to reply. I knew he loved me, though.

The wind rose and the dark gathered around the three of us. There was no snow falling. Only a great silence.

We were all very close and very small.

I shuddered and felt my blood boil with pressure, like a thermometer suddenly rising.

There was nothing to do but wait for something we could not see, could not define. I felt very helpless, apprehensive. I didn't know what to expect, so I did nothing. One cannot hide from such apprehensions. One can't defend against the unknown forces of nature.

So we just waited and listened for something that made no sound.

Later, a storm would come.

~ A Silent World ~

We had been snowed in for three days when we decided to try to trudge through the drifts to Ollinger's for some groceries. We bundled Colin up in a red snowsuit, put mittens on him, and set out with the sled for the store. There wasn't a track to be seen and it was still snowing. The flakes tore at our eyes when a gust of wind blew and fell gently when the wind died down. Our footprints were quickly obliterated and the going was slow in the deep drifts.

"Oh, Johnny, I love this," Angela said. "It's like being in a pure white secret world. I want it to stay like this. Nobody can see us and we can't see anybody. Look at Colin. He looks like a little frozen snowman."

"Not even cold, really."

"It's warm." She smiled. "Truly warm. I feel alive inside, toasty and warm."

I'd seldom seen her so happy. The snow world seemed to bring the color to her cheeks, brighten her laugh, warm her smile. Little Colin was wide-eyed with wonder, tasting the snow on his tongue, watching the swirling flakes all around him.

The walk seemed to be endless. It was like being in a tunnel. We couldn't see very far ahead. Each step was like going into another separate world.

Certain things changed, but the snow was the leitmotif of all the small enclosed white worlds. Silence was the contrapuntal melody.

We hadn't had a winter like that in a long time. Angela was

from Michigan and I from Minnesota, originally. But Southern California had been our home for many years.

Walking through the miniblizzard that day made us into children again. Colin was our age, we were his age. We made the walk last a long time. We had a childhood to recapture in the falling snow.

We didn't want to grow up again.

Red-cheeked and loaded down with groceries on the sled, we finally came back to our chalet. We were snowed in there for another two days.

"I hope it never stops snowing," Angela said, just before the snow stopped.

We made the winter last a long time.

~ *Images of Pinewood Lake* ~

You ask me if Pinewood Lake really exists.

It does, but mostly in the mind. The people are all real, once in a while; at other times, they are floating shapes of protoplasm from an unseen plane of existence just outside the periphery of normal vision.

When we first came here, we thought everything and everyone was real. At that time the village, the valley, the people, were all clearly defined. The folks were linear, in perfect position, all in their correct places on the grand layout. A was on square 1, B was on square 2, etc.

But these initial images were all rather deceptive, probably, three-dimensional shapes translated into reality by my own wishes. But we felt safe. I think that the valley here presents a face to newcomers that is masked. We received what we expected: a quiet, friendly place with settled, friendly people, an image of people being people. We reflected the same image.

We were accepted. We accepted.

One doesn't look too closely at a good thing.

Pinewood Lake was better than anything we had seen in a long time.

Look closely, though; scrutinize carefully, and images change.

Images are only images, after all, and open to interpretation by the beholder. Images are fragmented views of what we want to see as whole ideas, fully realized.

We saw Pinewood Lake as we wished to see it. We saw its

people as fractionated images of ourselves—an odd mistake, but not an unnatural one.

We see what we want to see, sometimes; at others, we see what we must.

In the lake here, we finally saw many other images, all true, all distorted, fragmented or all clear—but all merely images. Virtual reality, so to speak. Digital landscapes based on computer codes, programmed by our minds.

Reflections of ourselves, of others, of worlds here and now, of past and future times, places.

There is a star somewhere far out in this elastic cosmos that is recording the history of our planet. Our light has traveled there at 186,000 miles per second.

By the time our images reach this star we are already dead. We are only images.

By the time you read this, the author and his people may not exist.

Pinewood Lake is real at this moment.

It is, however, only an image. I am giving you fragments—the way life is truly seen and lived.

These are fragments of the image, parts of the truth.

There is not enough paper in the world to give you the whole truth about any person, any town. There is not enough time to do more than show you some few photographs, some hasty sketches, an entry or two from a diary.

Everything that happens is shot out into space, reflected off this planet like light from a lake. Someone, some being somewhere, may have the full story.

Someone knows that Pinewood Lake is real, that it exists. That someone will not be precisely certain when all the events recorded here occurred in this vast universe, nor why, but they will know that they did happen. So will you.

Someone, and you, will see Pinewood's images, its pulsating fragments trickling through time and space.

Pinewood Lake is a real place. Parts of it are here on these pages. Other parts are in your mind, in your dreams, in your karmic past.

It's just a small town in the universe. People built it, people can destroy it.

Its images and essences, however, are deathless.

Part Two

~ The Spring ~

And the spring comes slowly up this way.
—Samuel Taylor Coleridge
"Christabel"

~ *Spring* ~

One day there were six-foot drifts outside our house. Then the sun began shining during the day and the snow melted. Every night it froze, so it took the snow a long time to melt. We waited for our tulip bulbs to sprout. They were in no hurry to push up through the earth, or so it seemed.

The lake stayed frozen over for a long time, too. When the ice finally gave way there was a huge thundercrack. It sounded like distant cannon fire. In the mists I could see battles fade away, think of my ancestors in the Civil War.

All of this was our spring, shrugging its shoulders like a bewildered child.

I was very excited and unable to write much. I could envision the trout like sunken dirigibles waiting for my line to seek them out. I knew where they were: over at Sansone's Trailer Park on the north shore. The sun hit there all day long and the water ran first in that spot.

As soon as there was enough open water, I went over there with a fisherman named Smiley Pike. I had met him at the Kaos during the winter and he told me we would catch rainbows there. The docks went out a ways from the shore and we could fish through the ice. We took some beer along and newspapers to read. It was still cold and we had to go back to the car to warm up every once in a while.

We caught trout, all right, just like Smiley said. We lost one in the ice, snaking him across. It was Smiley's fish. He flopped there a long time before the ice melted and he fell through, back into the lake.

Smiley has lived here for several years. He's a bachelor. Short crew-cut hair, about fifty, he's from Minnesota. He works only to hunt and fish. It is a very trying time for him. He hunts ducks and is shot more often by hunters than not. He gets a few ducks, though. Smiley never keeps any of the game he takes. He gives the fish and the ducks away. Sometimes people invite him over for dinner. But not very often. He is a loner, but he's friendly.

We caught ten trout apiece and were the first fishermen on the lake that spring.

The trout looked like shrunken zeppelins, silvery and pink as though the sun had touched them for a moment after we landed them.

I went home with twenty trout and Colin thought I was a hero. Angela cooked them in Sauterne and drank some of it herself. They were very delicious, but Smiley couldn't stay for supper. He had to go down to the Kaos and be alone.

~ *Our Flowers* ~

The bulbs we planted last fall became flowers.
Tulips and crocuses and hyacinths. Our yard blazed and
pulsed with them. They were soft and delicate and fiery with life.

That's what I like about these kinds of flowers here. They
embody qualities that are superhuman, although naturalists
would question my premise. I have seen our flowers laugh and cry,
become despondent, manic, responsive to love. Like people garbed
in green with gaily colored hats.

Our yard was pretty bare the previous year without them.

Angela and I used to walk down the street to the village and
see other people's flowers. We were envious. So we bought some
bulbs that first fall at Ollinger's Store. We bought some bonemeal
and followed the directions, planted them so many inches deep.
Then it snowed and we wondered if they were warm in the
ground, full of dreams. I thought of them all winter, thought of
them as heavy thick eggs that needed only spring to make them
crack open.

It was a long winter for the bulbs and for me.

I worried about them.

When they came up, both Angela and I were excited. Tough
green shoots pushing through the snow. It kept snowing and
snowing, sporadically, but enough to keep the ground white.
Finally it stopped snowing and the shoots really began to move.

They kept raising up to the sun, getting fatter and fatter.

The first blooms were even more exciting to us. We were

awed by this phenomenon in our yard. Everywhere we had planted a bulb, a flower sprouted. We were on hand at a minor creation.

Then the neighbors' dogs came. They ran through our yard and always seemed to plant their splayed feet on the tender shoots struggling for survival. It was hell watching some of the flowers being destroyed by the senseless roamings of those terrible dogs.

Most of the crocuses and hyacinths and tulips survived this onslaught.

Next fall, I vowed, I would plant more bulbs. I would make a fence of tulips, a fiery warning to all intruders that this yard was ours and nature's. I would make a barrier so that the dogs would have to carry machetes in order to cut their way through our yard. They would drown in flowers if they came this way. They would surely drown in another kind of love.

~ Angela Sleeping ~

The dark worlds of sleep around us. Angela beside me in the upstairs bedroom, curled up, lost in her secret torment. I didn't know which way to go. I looked out the window and saw our car dying, its white hulk glazed by moonlight. I had kept it together with thousands of dollars. I had kept myself together with writing, with dreaming.

I tried to talk to her.

I tried to explain things that were churning inside me: how to grow plants and live off the land; how to work together with the talents we had; how to be honest and try for fineness in ourselves; how to raise our child to know consideration, responsibility, and love. All complex, vast, like the problems of the lake full of carp and weeds. They put a bounty of ten cents on each carp so kids would kill them. This failed. They have tried various poisons and de-weeding methods for the weeds—all failures.

I was a failure with Angela. By now it was certain that she was an alcoholic and this place, away from the big city, was a hotbed for alcoholics. They grow out of dark places like diseased mushrooms, filling the bars with their empty raucous laughter. They fear the day and wear dark glasses. Their hands tremble in the mornings. Their sleeps are full of horrible apparitions. They inhabit the land with terrible unsolvable burdens. They sleep in dark worlds unknown to the rest of us, wrapped in blankets of snakes and large black Frankenstein parables.

Angela pulsed in her sleep like the dying Cadillac. Her face was tawdry white in the moonlight, paled and sharpened by an inner tenseness. I turned away from the window and looked at her, perfecting a simile. I could not fix either one: the machine or the soul of the sleeping woman. I could not relate to either.

Downstairs, I wrote a few words in my diary. They were meaningless in the face of the reality. I was in love with a woman who was not human anymore. She drank secretly, draining all of us there in that house and that land of energy, of love. Colin slept in his crib and I wondered if he knew or sensed what we both had lost.

The lake was out there, by itself, oblivious to those things. That night, in my incredible sadness, it seemed full of a million tears I could not shed. It was very quiet, full of muffled guitars, full of the sad eyes of drunken women, full of the quiet hearts of men, the frowns of troubled children.

The lake was full of unwritten diaries, full of the dark worlds of sleep where indescribable shapes floated at various levels like apparitions from another universe.

~ The Oaks ~

The oaks had turned green. In the sun, against the blue sky, they were like a fountain of emeralds. I looked at them, out my window, and dreamed of my summer boyhood. They were very comfortable to look at. I wish Colin could know how I felt about those trees in spring. I wish Angela could have felt about them the way I did.

The sun turned their leaves different shades of viridian. The shadows conspired to make up a composite of greennesses, all of a single piece, yet separate, as though each leaf were fashioned from different cloth, in different perspective. The branches of those trees moved in all directions, like satellites, slow-growing, peaceful in their positions.

I could almost see the sap feeding the veins of the leaves, surging through the branches.

Oh, Colin, Angela, I thought. "Look quick, before it's too late," I wanted to shout.

I couldn't have painted these trees for you. Yet they have painted themselves.

~ *The Old Logger* ~

Merle Dodd made the table in our living room. It is a beauti-ful creation. The wood is from the last large cedar in the forest. Merle, a lumberjack from the Northwest, makes his living from the woods. He is an adviser to the U.S. Department of Agriculture and a consultant for a major chainsaw firm. He is a big man with scarred and nicked hands who wears bright red suspenders emblazoned with the name of the chainsaw firm he represents in advertisements.

The table is our proudest possession. It is six feet long, four inches thick. Two benches, made from the same huge cedar, make a perfect accompaniment to its beauty. Merle sands the wood, pours resin in the wide cracks, polishes it lovingly again, and then encases the wood in a film of tough acrylic.

"Don't never use a furniture polish on this wood," he told us.

He was right. The table, with its dark and its golden fibers, dominates the huge living room—dining room like a baron's table. The legs are made from the cedar trunk itself, split in halves to give a solid foundation to the masterpiece.

Merle places ads in swingers' publications to assure himself of female companionship during the long winters. He always has a different guest at his home. His home is filled with objects he has carved from trees. In his years of lumberjacking he grew to love the forest and, like an artist, saw sculptures within the wood. He still does, although he is old and the woods he knew are all gone, swallowed up and pulped by Weyerhauser, Scott, and the like. Someday a tree will fall wrong and smash old Merle while he's rattling that chainsaw he helped design. The tree will be huge and it will make no sound because no one will be there to hear it.

We will think of Merle, as we always do, as being in those old photographs where a bunch of tiny humans in overalls are standing underneath a monster tree that they will fell with a two-handed buck saw long before Stihl, McCullough, and Homelite ever existed.

We thank God that Teddy Roosevelt kept these hearty strapping lads out of Yellowstone and Yosemite. We wonder, though, when some Secretary of Agriculture will turn the horde loose on the national forests with savage chainsaws in their hands, bringing the old giants down—trees that have lived on earth since before the time of the pharaohs and seen it all from their mighty towers and recorded it in their graceful and mysterious rings, secrets that can be unlocked only when their flesh is severed and their torsos bared in death, their existence reduced to stumps where a man might sit and weep at the loss without shade, without the cool bower of leaves overhead.

Old Merle came over one day looking like a thin grizzly bear.

He was terribly hung over. One of his eyes was bigger than the other. It also had more pink in the white part. The smaller eye was almost shut. His jowls hung down. I thought he had forgotten his teeth, but when I offered him a chew of Beech-Nut, he took a few scraggly leaves out of the pouch and stuffed it into his mouth. I could see his teeth way back as if they had been bent there by a fist.

"I got popped last night," he said. "Drove my teeth back."

"How come?" I asked.

"I don't know. I got on a toot. Don't do that much anymore. Went to the Kaos and to Pluto's, down to Archers. Blew a lot of money. Some guy popped me at Big Ossie's. After that I don't remember."

"I didn't think you drank," I told him.

"Don't. Can't. I quit when I came up here. Do it every once in a while. Lost my wallet somewhere. Had all my money in it."

Angela came downstairs then and Merle looked at her pitifully, as though he had been kicked by an invisible foot.

"Hi, Merle," she said politely.

I offered him a beer but he refused it. He took some Copenhagen from an overall pocket and pinched off a bit and stuck it behind his lip. Mixed with the Beech-Nut. I looked at him with envy. Here was a real tobacco chewer.

"These bastards up here don't know how to take care of the trees," he said. "I could show 'em in a minute how to save 'em. They keep talking about pine beetles. Hell, I planted pine beetles and bad knots in many trees that I wanted to fall for my business."

We wondered what Old Merle wanted as he droned on about the stupidity of the Forest Service and the people who planted pine trees as useless ecological gestures.

"I could save the trees," he said again, "and bring back the deer."

"Great," I said. "We'll write a book about it."

"Only thing," he chomped, "I can't stay away from liquor and women." He got up then, spat a wad of tobacco juice into a cup I'd given him, and walked out the door, a big lumbering hulk.

Merle wasn't hung over anymore.

~ The Old Car ~

The old Cadillac had gone dead like an automotive manual fallen in the rain, soaked and swollen from the water, the time.

I had tried to stem the obsolescence, keep from performing euthanasia on the machine that brought us here to Pinewood Lake.

The money to keep the car alive had run out. Cars are built that way by Detroit. They keep you going long enough to get broke keeping them together, running, then they die and become tombstones, reminding you and your creditors about the promise of luxury for people who never have enough money.

Like us.

I kept writing, though, and my wife, Angela, made bread from whole wheat flour. We felt close to the earth. We could smell the land all over America in the baking of this bread. We could smell the ovens of our ancestors, think of their wagon tracks across the land a hundred years ago. We could sense wheat and corn and barley growing in the great plains where the rain rings like wind chimes on summer afternoons.

I saw the pages of my old car peel off, words and thoughts stripped away by the rain. I could feel an old watch ticking down, losing its spring. Old payment records blew away in the wind, yellow receipts crackled like leaves in a quiet fire. It was a kind of autumn of automobiles and I could see them all dangling there on branches of life in cities all over America, finally falling junky in the yards of poverty or carelessness, turning rust in the autumn of men and women like dreams in Technicolor just before dawn.

The arthritic wires; crumpled, worn out tires; and the seats of leather that held us for so long, now sag and bag in silence in the yard. We were too poor to move the hulk to a junkyard, too stoned on life to accomplish the final kill of our car.

The car just sat there like a grotesque statue of another era, white as bone, gaunt as the moon on its last huddle from the big shadow of its waning, like new, like old, like nothing.

Well, this happens. Cars die like people. It doesn't mean much.

I could still hear the Caddie hum, though, out there in the moonyard. I could hear its whining though its heart was dead and rusted and locked into a time we didn't know anymore. I could hear its motor throb in the keys of my typewriter, whiff its gas, see the road streak out ahead of me through all the graveyards of Automobile America.

~ Dinner with Friends ~

Lorraine Goldman came over one night for dinner with Tommy Elmo and Katherine Marceau. Peter was supposed to come, but had the flu, Lorraine said. Angela was not drinking, so it was a nice evening for all of us. I made beef stroganoff and served it over rice. We had red wine and B & Bs afterward.

Lorraine brought some of her poetry. It was well written, but had been published five years ago in a college journal. She said she was still writing poetry and wanted to know all about publishing in the literary magazines. I told her how to go about it.

She read some of my poetry and didn't say anything. No comment. No comment. No comment.

Kathy talked about metaphysical things. Tommy told some spooky stories. After a while we all went outside and looked up at the stars.

Lorraine took some food home for Peter. She raved about my cooking. Over and over, incessantly.

Well, I thought, I can't turn her on with poetry, but the way to her heart is through her stomach.

We invited Peter and Lorraine over often after that, but they never came.

Tommy and Kathy came over a lot. They brightened our lives. We had several of Kathy's paintings in our home and some of Tommy's silk screens. The paintings were made of earth and flowers and light. Sometimes a horse danced across a moonlit meadow sniffing the flowers. The silk screens were abstracts of butterfly like images, or gaily colored Rorschachs. They were at once intensely gloomy and wildly gay. I liked them very much. They were like Tommy, who was always laughing, but who seemed to be bearing a hidden sadness. Kathy was ebullient but her sadness was not hidden. It hung around her eyes like old cobwebs.

Sometimes Angela and I would look at Kathy's paintings and feel sunshine or moonlight, depending on which time of day she had depicted. With Tommy's silk screens we always felt like we were being haunted by an unknown presence.

"I think Kathy's paintings are growing," Angela said to me one day. "They give me a creepy feeling. I'm afraid they might turn real and kill us."

"That's silly, Angela."

"You always think I'm silly, Johnny. You don't believe I have any brains."

"That's not true."

"Yes, it is. Sometimes you look at me as if I'm an idiot. You don't really know that I have feelings, that I have thoughts. Just like you do."

"Angela, please."

"See?" she said.

Lorraine's poems are shriveling up on the yellow pages of her school's journal. She'd never be able to paint those growing things on our walls or to see them for what they were and where they came from.

~ Doctor Stoval ~

Y our wife's an acute alcoholic," said Dr. Marvin Stoval, the
town doctor. He had given Angela a complete physical after
her last three-day drunk. "She's a progressive alcoholic."

"What's that mean?"

"Every drink she takes hits her harder, deteriorates her faster.
Her liver's damaged."

"But she never had any problems before. Not until we came
here," I added bitterly.

"That's why we call it progressive. She probably drank
socially for years. Then, gradually, it crept up on her. Now she
can't handle alcohol at all. Her system's allergic to it."

"She may be allergic to it, but she's drawn to it, too."

"That's one of the symptoms," he said. Stoval was a young
man, in his thirties, with a mop of curly hair that made him look
like Harpo Marx. Yet there was an intelligence in his eyes, a
concern.

I stood up, confused.

"Is there anything I can do?" I asked him. "Anything you
can do?"

"She can't handle alcohol, Johnny. There are some people here
who may be able to help."

He gave me a list of telephone numbers. Hieroglyphics. I was
a stranger here, with Angela even more a stranger now that an
invisible barrier between us and the world had become visible.

"She wasn't like this before," I said, still unable to understand

Stoval. "She says she likes it here, yet she's destroying us, our home."

"That's a symptom. She'll get worse. Even if she stops drinking for ten years, then takes another one, the progression will still be there. There is no cure."

"It's not Pinewood Lake, is it? What triggered it? I mean, it just doesn't make sense."

"No, it doesn't make sense. But she had this long before you came here. Try to understand, Johnny."

Try to understand? I went home and looked at Angela. She was changing Colin's diaper. She looked just fine. I told her what Dr. Stoval had said. She was calm, but her eyes filled with tears.

"I know," she said.

"You mean you know you're an alcoholic?"

"Yes."

I was dumbfounded.

"How long have you known?" I asked her.

"Since I was eighteen," she said.

"But you never got drunk. You always handled it."

"Until now. But I knew I was an alcoholic by the time I had my second drink."

I looked at her. She seemed far away just then.

"How—how did you know?" I stammered.

She looked at me with an odd expression on her face.

"By the way it made me feel," she said. "I felt very strange all over."

I shuddered with a sudden chill when she said that. Somehow, I knew what she meant.

Colin smiled up at her and she looked, for an instant, like an angel playing her harp.

~ Fishing Alone ~

The lake was a pure reflection of dawn: pristine, calm, roseate with a tranquility like a quiet crane stalking a shore of earth. These spring mornings are devastating to a writer. It is impossible to work carefully when you can take a breath full of sunshine and see the lake beckoning. In the north country of Minnesota, or in the high lakes of Colorado, trout and bass would be leaping for the insects dancing over the still waters. Here, at Pinewood Lake, the lake is pure glass, undisturbed.

I toss my line out and break the surface tension. The treble hooks baited with floating cheese, an egg sinker, flow from a yellow pole and a reel guaranteed for life. I know the channel in the lake where the big rainbows lurk. Blop. My sinker disturbs the sheeted steel of the water, rumples the blue-pink integument.

Then, morning is electric. I dance a trout through the weeds and shallows, bring him to shore. He is fourteen inches long. He weighs a pound and a half. He is beautiful. He is a female, full of eggs that will never be spawned.

Angela is at home today, with Colin. I can see the sunshine pouring in the windows. I can imagine their eyes when I bring home trout for a meal this evening. I can see her guarding him like a dark-maned lioness, see her change his diapers, prepare his bottles, talk about Daddy who has gone fishing.

My metal stringer fills up. I have five trout, dying in the shallows, their rainbow colors fading. I wish Matisse were here, or Cézanne. They could handle these colors, these elusive flashes of nickel, lilac, and case-hardened steel. They could catch me on the bank as I snake the trout in on a four-pound test line, my pole jiggling.

I wish they were here with me at these moments, Angela and Colin. I wish they could see me returning to my heritage, my ancestral urgings, my primitive beginnings. I wish they could see how I wait when the pole starts to tremble, how I hook our supper with a deft jerk of the pole, a quick wind of the reel. I wish they could see how much I love them in my old shape on the shore.

I wish they could see me catch the pink steel dawn on a golden hook.

~ *The Prisoner* ~

Angela didn't make it that time.

She had been drinking for five days. What was left of her real personality had been drowned by alcohol. Her brain was functioning like a saturated sponge. No signals were going out or coming in. She hadn't eaten. Her body was twisted in pain and her eyes were unseeing. She was very pitiful to look at.

The people from Alcoholics Anonymous came over.

"She should go to the hospital," said Marianne, who had been there before, around the Horn, up the creek, and all over hell with booze.

"You should take her down to the alky ward," said Marianne's companion on the twelve-step call, Dan. They never use last names in AA, but Angela knew these people. In a small town like that it was impossible to be anonymous.

"I can't take her," I said. "She tried to jump out of the car before when I wanted to get help for her. I've got Colin here."

"We'll take her down," said Dan, a florid-faced man who used to drink heavily and now fights the temptation on a day-to-day basis.

"I'd be very grateful," I said.

"They'll keep her seventy-two hours for observation," said Marianne, a sylph-like creature who didn't look as though she could handle anything stronger than mother's milk or formula in a baby bottle. But she had been a hard drinker from the time she was fourteen until a year ago. She was only twenty-three now. She said she'd always started out with a six-pack of beer, then went on to vodka or wine. Learned it from her father.

Right then, Marianne and Dan both looked like angels of mercy to me. Angela was babbling that she wouldn't go.

"You might have trouble," I told Dan.

"We've had trouble before," he said. "We'll be back to pick her up in a half hour. I have to make arrangements to go down the hill."

"Okay."

In a half hour they were back. Angela went with them docilely. She was fine until they got her to the admissions office of the county hospital. She ran, she screamed, she lied. She almost convinced the doctors that she was being railroaded. She was very clever, like most alcoholics. Marianne told me that they had gotten her admitted. I was sick. She had fallen a long way.

Colin and I were two unlikely bachelors for three days. Those were three days cut out of my life, like part of a heart. For Angela, it was much worse.

She was a prisoner.

~ *Dan* ~

I asked Dan to explain Angela to me. He said he'd try.

"She's just like the rest of us," he said. "The booze caught up with her. No more social boozing. She's an alky forever. She'll get worse every time she takes a drink. She's got to lay off, period."

"But she was never that way before," I explained.

Dan laughed, his face a landscape of crimson flowers.

"None of us were, Johnny. Angela's got a kind of poison in her system. She craves the stuff but it's dynamite for her. She'll dry out a little down there in the alky ward, get scared, but she'll forget all about that the next time she wants a drink."

"What can be done?"

"Get her on the program—if she wants to. We meet twice a week. Read the literature I'll leave you. It's a long slow haul."

"I don't care. Angela's too good to waste like this. I'm picking her up tomorrow."

"Good. Have a long talk. She should have some insights now. Bring her to AA. It's no miracle place and there's no cure for what she's got. But we try to help each other."

"I know, Dan. I'm very grateful."

He left then. I looked through the leaflets he left. "The Alcoholic Husband," "The Alcoholic Wife." They included everyone but the baby, but the material made sense.

Dan looked okay to me. He hadn't had a drink in two years.

His face looked like a peeled peach sometimes. You could see the veins where alcohol had ravaged his complexion.

Angela wasn't like that yet. She wasn't a two-fisted bar drinker. I tried to console myself.

Angela was a secret drinker. She lived in her own private hell. No one had been able to reach her. No one had tried before.

~ The Growing Things ~

A ngela was very excited when the bulbs we planted started to come through. She scurried here and there, pointing out the green shoots in the wet earth.

"Isn't this great?" she said. "They're coming up."

"Didn't you expect them to?"

"Yes, but they're ours, Johnny. They're ours. Like our own little babies."

Colin toddled around, wondering what all the excitement was about. This was a good place to grow. A good place to learn about such things. He was too small to understand much, but he learned a new word for plants. "Pants, pants," he called them.

Every time he saw a bulb shoot coming up, he said, "Pant."

He was learning about nature.

We were already planning a vegetable garden. It was still March, but we ordered seed catalogs anyway. The locals all said you couldn't plant until late April or early May, but I could hardly wait. I could already see rows of peas, beans, tall corn, melons on the vine, tomatoes on plush bushes, bell peppers, radishes, lettuce, thick clumps of spinach.

Angela was just as crazy as I, and for a while I thought she was really going to pull out of it. She did like the land up here, was happy with her home. Night after night we made lists of vegetables we wanted to order. She seemed very content. We showed Colin pictures in the Gurney's seed catalog and named all the fruits and vegetables for him. He could pronounce some of them. He liked the colored pictures.

We wanted Colin to know about growing things.

We hoped he would grow up in that fine land, knowing the value of life in all its forms. He was very precious to us.

He seemed to be part of the earth and the flora of the forest, growing just like a "pant." We nurtured him with our love. We poured it over him every day, each night when we tucked him in his bed.

The bulbs bloomed and so did our son. He was the Little Prince among the plants, running in and out of their rows with glee.

"Grow, grow," we told the bulbs.

"Go, go," said Colin, knowing what we meant.

He was the highest tulip in our small garden.

~ *Indian Talk* ~

Angela was the important substance.

She glistened here and there like a diamond in a mud bank. I wanted to discover her, pick her up, and carry her home. She was anchored well, like all good things. Hard to pick up. Hard to polish, to make gleaming. Valuable, nonetheless.

I saw her one day, looking like an Indian.

She looked out over the garden with no flash of eyes. She was like a weaver spellbound with her weaving, a Penelope returned to sanity at dawn. Her eyes were very brown, like mine, though they were usually shot with amber. The amber was a thing of pain, something close to a nugget in stone getting sun very early in the day.

She was very solemn.

The garden was too dry that morning.

The leaves of the plants were gray and wilting, like Angela.

I had to get the hose out and turn it on. I sprayed the garden. It turned green and glistening all of a sudden.

The Lakota language came back to me. I spoke to Angela in ragged Sioux. "How cola. Wacincila cistila." A little girl staring out at a greening garden, looking like a lost Indian. I made some sign language. Many things growing under the sun. Good earth. Good woman.

Angela turned to me with brown eyes, blooming.

I sprayed her with the hose and she laughed like a garden watered. I tossed my head like a fountain.

I polished a diamond sunk in mud.

~ Cries over the Lake ~

There were far cries over the lake.

They were like the cries of lost children. The bars were ringing with false laughter, keenings of the dying.

It was a sad night.

"I wonder what that sound is," said Angela.

"Coyotes. Kids playing," I answered.

"No, not that. Someone's being murdered. Someone's in trouble."

"We're in trouble, Angela."

"What did you say?"

"Never mind. It wasn't important."

Someone had written our dialogue. Nunnally Johnson. Dalton Trumbo. Alvah Bessie. F. Scott Fitzgerald. We were in a movie, trapped on a flickering screen. The credits had rolled and it was sunset with nothing happening. Just dialogue.

Angela gave me her profile and I adjusted the light. The meter trebled its needle. A whistle blew. Sound! Speed! Cut!

Mumbles of the actress, Angela.

Onion juice in my eyes. Far cries over the lake.

"We have to go a long way," she said, I thought.

"Yes. Over to the other side?"

"To this side."

"That doesn't make sense, Angela."

"I'm very tired and I wonder what's going on over there."

"The same thing that's going on over here. People. Action."

She turned her profile as the barn doors opened to give her light. A baby spot illumined her brown eyes.

"Nothing's going on over here," she said. "It's as if all three of us are dead and don't know it yet. I feel like I'm in a tomb."

Then close cries ringing over the lake. Something was going on. Angela and I and all the things in between.

It was like a sweet willing rape.

Cut and print.

~ Suspicion ~

Angela was very suspicious of me, of Dan, and of Marianne when she got back home. She sat for three days writing down her terrible experiences in the alcoholic ward. There were people there who had delirium tremors. There were schizophrenics there. It was not a place she belonged. I felt guilty having been a party to her three-day commitment.

"I wasn't that drunk," she told me.

"You were not yourself, Angela."

"You should have seen the other people down there. Sodden. Like animals. Wretches, all of them. Ugly people with ugly problems. Small, mean people, stinking of whiskey and beer."

"They don't interest me. I love you. I thought maybe the place would impress on you the seriousness of your disease."

"I don't have to be locked up like a madwoman to understand that," she said. "I'll be all right now. You're the only therapy I need. Really. I'm all right when I'm with you. When I don't have to deal with shallow people, unwholesome people."

She cried whenever she thought about that ward down the hill.

I had picked up an old broken woman. She was trembling with fear and indignation. She had a right to her temporary paranoia from what I'd heard about the place. She had to eat with a tablespoon. Attendants had to light her cigarette. She had to sit in a corridor all day with sad people, some of them demented, brains boiled by alcohol or seared by drugs.

"Colin was very insecure while you were gone," I told her. "He missed you."

"I missed him, too. I thought I'd never see him again. I thought it was all part of a vicious kidnapping plan to keep me away from my son." She wept again, thinking of that.

"We missed you, Angela. Stay with us."

"I will," she said.

She was with us for a month, going to AA meetings, brightening up like a spring day.

Then she got drunk, for no reason I could determine.

There was no place to send her, though. She lived in a claustrophobic world of her own. I took Colin over to the Elmos' and just let Angela drink herself down into her pit. She poured the vodka down, ate crackers and peanut butter, fell against the furniture, down the stairs. She was smashed for three days, then she came out of it. Her stomach hurt horribly. Her hair was straggly, her body a mass of ugly purple bruises.

"I don't trust you anymore," I told her when she was sober. "I'm very suspicious of you now. You're very destructive."

"I'm suspicious of you, too, Johnny. You're ready to have me locked up again."

"No, that's not true."

Angela was already locked up in some dark castle keep where goblins and demons prowled.

And no one had the key to let her out.

~ *Limbo* ~

S pring became a kind of limbo.

Angela drifted in and out of our lives like part of a song you can't quite remember, can't get right in your mind. Colin seemed to sense the changes. He was vocal about it with his limited vocabulary.

"Mommie sleepin'," he said, his mother curled up like a mindless fetus on the chair.

He and I revolved around her, though, like displaced satellites in a state of chaos, constantly changing orbits.

She was taking us somewhere, to an unknown destination. It was almost summer. We were eating fresh radishes from our garden. The turnips and carrots couldn't fight their way to root in the rocky soil. Peas flourished and the spinach managed. The robins and jays ate the tomatoes while they were still green. The squirrels snipped off the tiny strawberries just for the hell of it.

"If you want strawberries," Merle had told me, "you go down to Ollinger's and put them in your shopping basket."

It was very discouraging.

Where was Angela taking us?

Through her own garden, to a hell that might have been painted by Hieronymus Bosch in a state of delirium.

Part Three

~ The Summer ~

'Tis just like a summer bird-cage in a garden:
the birds that are without despair to get in,
and the birds that are within despair and are
in a consumption for fear they shall never get out.
—John Webster
The White Devil

~ Group Portrait ~

There is no portrait of us anywhere.

No photographs.

We don't even own a camera. We are just three people living by the lake here. We could be anybody. We could be from any time in history.

I'm middle-aged, somewhat paunchy. Angela is thin and beautiful, dark with fearful eyes. Colin is towheaded and cute, like a child in an ad for baby food.

We are books and homemade bread, silhouettes by a winter fire, people stooped over a spring garden, fisherfolk on a summer shore. We are bright salads and beer, ice cream afternoons, a family at a once-a-week movie. We are silent strollers in the pines, picnickers up in Honeycomb Valley, boaters on a Sunday lake.

We are wanderers, transplanted nomads of California, explorers of the dim trails, the broken arrastres, the weathered boards of old sluices, the dark pits of abandoned mines. We are the autumn people lying on leaves in a forest glade, sleeping in the shade after lunch, the people typing early in the morning before Pinewooders go to work, the group together before a black-and-white television after dinner.

That's us: Angela, Colin, and Johnny. A whole bunch of people in a triumvirate, caught in time, living up here above the smog.

This is part of our only portrait.

It is a group portrait.

~ *Murdered* ~

We walked into the village, holding onto the sky before it became black.

Angela and I were going in to see a movie at the Pinewood Theater, owned by Bob and Thelma Monteval. We walked down our lane, Dogwood, up Stevens, turned right, and strolled along Washington Avenue down into the village. The street there is Pine Knot Boulevard. The movie house is right across the street from three bars, the Kaos, Pluto's Bar, and Archers, which once used to be an old stage stop.

To our right, the north, the lake moved between the pines, on the high parts of Washington, like a blue-veiled lady dancing at evening. I thought of the trout, deep-floating submarines, waiting in there for my cast. Angela squeezed my hand, bringing me back to her, a fish being played on an invisible line.

We didn't stop at any of the bars.

After the movie, Bob and Thelma picked us up on the way back home. We were grateful because it was very dark.

The movie had been violent and we were afraid.

That same night, a man was killed right on Pine Knot Boulevard. He was shot to death by an angry woman with a pistol she snatched out of her purse, so the story went. The woman fled. She was never seen again. No one ever knew who she was or why she did it. The man, a flatlander, had just moved up here. He was a stranger, too. His name was Michael Smith.

This was not our first experience with violence.

The first night here, we had sensed it, both of us. When Angela screamed outside our snow-driven house, we knew that anger could boil up here, even in the midst of these serene pines.

When we found out about the killing, we were very quiet for a few days. We paid special attention to Colin, who was very small, very sweet. We looked to him for help. We didn't want harm to come to him.

We didn't want harm to come to us.

The night sky became black a lot of times after that. We always wondered what caused it.

Usually we can see the stars, the planets, and the moon.

Usually we can see what's up there, above us, feel ourselves, rightly, down below, humble and curious.

~ *Condor Point* ~

The industry in Pinewood Lake is divided into two parts: tourism and real estate. There are many other businesses, of course, but these are the main two. Angela and I had no interest in either of them after we settled here last winter. We were in the business of summer and being on the lake.

Colin was very delighted with my catching bluegills. He was Saint-Exupéry's Little Prince, with his curly blond hair and his glittering eyes, tiny feet on the muddy shore. I caught these sunny fish on small hooks baited with worms and threw them into a bucket. They splashed him and he giggled before he ran away, only to return again and poke his finger into the bucket.

We liked to fish at a place east of Condor Point. There were a few houses around, big ones where people never came out except to throw their cocktail ice over the porches before going into the air-conditioned insides again. We ignored them haughtily as we munched on sandwiches and drank cold beer and colas between fishing expeditions.

I would wade into the lake, out past the big weeds. That's where I would catch the bluegills. It takes about twenty of them to make a meal for us and friends. We liked to soak them in milk-and-egg batter, dip them in cornmeal, and fry them. I like them with the heads on. But Angela couldn't stand to look at them that way, so I would leave the heads on until the last moment. Too bad, because they lose a lot of their flavor when you behead them.

I don't write much during the summer. It's no fun. Sometimes I would take my pad with me and write down things while I was waiting for the fish to bite, but once they started biting I didn't care if the paper got splashed, which it sometimes did. The business of summer was important to us that year. That's when we could be tourists without having to pay high fees or return to someplace far away after the weekend. That's when we could enjoy seeing people without having to bother with them. The tourists have their problems.

We liked to think we didn't have any.

One day, though, Angela began drinking down by Condor Point. The beer hit her hard. The sun may have helped her to get drunk. She got cloudy and puckered up like a storm. Colin began to scream and I had to quit fishing. I got a hook caught in my shirt. It nicked my skin. I slapped Angela for drinking so much. She was babbling and Colin was crying. His diaper was wet, too.

I caught only six bluegill that day. In our anger, we fed them to the cats and forgot about the business of summer and being on the lake. I put some Chopin music in the tape player and sulked the rest of the night while Angela snored against the hurt of evening. Colin lay in his crib with two bottles in his arms for security.

Not much real estate was sold that day.

~ The Diary ~

It is terrible to eavesdrop in someone's diary.

Angela wrote: "Johnny wants to get out of the rat race. That's why we're moving to Pinewood Lake. He wants to go there to write serious books. He doesn't like Los Angeles. It's okay with me. I hope he makes it. I think he will."

Another entry: "Johnny still has to write for the paying markets. He's working on a book in his spare time. He doesn't have any spare time. He works on it at night when he's tired. That's hard."

Later on: "We had a good day, but Johnny's very nervous. He can't make up his mind. We need the money he earns from the men's magazines and from the paperbacks, but he doesn't act like it's what he wants to do. His agent says the markets are all bad. It's depressing."

I'm sorry I ran across her diary. It is terrible to pry into private thoughts. I couldn't help reading it once I saw my name. Saw it often.

I went away, determined to change the future entries in her diary.

Hard to do.

There are so many fishermen up here, so many eager trout. There are so many pines in the woods making a path for me, so many excursions through the old mines, the country. It is a terrible place for a writer to live unless he's able to turn nature into dollars.

If I ate a wild berry or leaf, I'd probably be poisoned.

I forgot about the notebook until this moment. I kept writing the book. I kept watching Angela fall into the hell of alcoholism. I kept watching Colin learn to talk, learn to see. I kept wondering where I was, why I was, and how to make everything come together.

The words were right, here and there. I wrote letters to old poet friends. I got answers, sort of. They were all famous by then. I was still unknown, though highly paid for providing adventurous paperbacks loaded with sex to horny old men (as the cliché insists), articles for hairy-chested magazines, and short stories for some of the *Playboy* imitators.

There was tension in our household.

A new paper came into being: *The Pinewood News*. I started writing a column for it, ten bucks a shot. It was a good shot. Like adrenalin for me. I was able to get into the community, through my own eyes. I was able to put down what I felt about the country. It was my own diary. I didn't have to eavesdrop on Angela's anymore.

I wrote my heart out: I put it out there for all the community to see.

It lay there like a piece of liver in a butcher's window, ignored, as the flies swarmed over it, as it shriveled in the heat, hardened like some cirrhotic display, and sat there for a year with my very blood keeping it barely alive.

This was my own diary.

It was terrible for people to eavesdrop and ignore it.

I knew how they felt.

~ Confusion ~

Angela was drunk, very drunk. I had never seen anyone that stoned. She hadn't had that much to drink, or at least I hadn't noticed her having that much. We were at a party at Katherine Marceau's, the artist. Her husband, Tommy Elmo, who did silk screens, was putting away the beer, guzzling it down. Lorraine, the aspiring poet, and Peter Goldman, the architect, were also there. Angela got hit hard by the wine they had served and she began to grow hysterical after dinner.

She raved about the dead man, Smith, saying she had killed him.

"That's not true," Kathy said.

Angela began to weep.

"I killed my husband, too," she said. "I shot him dead with his pistol."

"She's just drunk," I said.

"They haven't found out who killed Smith," said Peter, who talked like a prosecutor. "The sheriffs think it was a woman."

"I killed him," Angela wept.

"Bullshit," said Tommy, always the practical one. He was from South Carolina and didn't miss much. He was less simple than people took him for. Kathy was psychic. She began to vibrate. Her face took on an aura, shining with some mysterious light. I had seen this same light in her paintings. It was eerie.

"Angela's first husband, a guy named Al Leeds, was killed in a parachute jump," I told them. "Angela wasn't even there."

Angela shot me a dirty look. Her face had changed into an evil witch's. It was distorted with fear and hatred. Her eyes were wild, uncertain. I felt very sorry for her.

I sat back, hoping she wouldn't be encouraged by Peter, a roly-poly young man who wore thick glasses and looked like Benjamin Franklin. Lorraine sipped her wine, waiting like a snake for blood to spill. Kathy glowed like an electric light bulb. Tommy smacked his lips.

Angela continued to weep, sobbing out a story of how she took a pistol and shot Smith because he had found out about her murdering her husband. I wanted to shake her, to pound some sense into her, but I held back. There was some psychic disturbance there that had to come out.

"She can't even shoot a gun," I put in.

"Interesting," said Peter. "Maybe she's confessing."

I wanted to smack the bastard.

"Let's go, Angela," I said. "You're drunk."

She screamed at me: "I'm not drunk! You're drunk! All of you! I'm telling you what happened. I killed them. I shot both of them!"

Kathy became very nervous. Lorraine stretched out her neck and leaned forward. She was sitting cross-legged on the floor. She was very thin and tall, serpentine, with glittering blue eyes that seemed half mad from the wine.

We were all mad, I decided. For sitting here watching a woman split apart, open her wounds to us.

"My wife's an alcoholic," I said. "She doesn't know what she's saying. I have to take her home."

Kathy came to Angela and put her arm around her shoulders. Angela burst into a deluge of sobbing, out of control. Tommy smacked his lips and slugged down a swallow of beer. Lorraine hunched forward, about to strike. Peter looked through his thick bifocals and sensed the drama they would all miss if I took Angela home.

"Good night," I said. "Thanks. She'll be all right in the morning."

I got Angela to her feet. She staggered against me, a torn little girl, very frail. We went outside, leaving the people with their anarchistic thoughts and wine-wise talk.

The moon was up full. I had heard it could to things to people, make them crazy, pull the tides in their veins like trapped seas, burst against the walls of the brain, smash against the vein barriers like surf against boulders.

The fresh air struck us and I got Angela into the car.

We drove home with the moon shining in the car window.

I carried her upstairs and put her to bed without undressing her. She fell asleep and tossed all night while I lay awake thinking about what she had said. It was crazy but I wondered where she got the urge to take on all that guilt.

The next morning, I asked her about what she had said. "You said you killed Al," I told her. "And that guy Smith, too."

"That's crazy," she said. "Why would I do anything like that?"

~ *Living in the Mountains* ~

Below us, seven thousand feet down, cities sprawl like smog-breathing tarantulas, dark-dayed villages, gray communities, choked towns of modern civilization. We left these conglomerate towns, these factories of progress pricetagged with emphysema, strangulation, death. We came here for survival, Angela, Colin, and I. We came here to breathe the clean clear fresh air of the mountains.

Other people had been here, too. We have found arrowheads and pieces of earthen pottery. The Serrano Indians, they say, used to summer here. Their children played games by the old dry lake and up in Honeycomb Valley, down here where the Pinewood sprawls. Then women raised corn and pounded it into mash, tasted its sweetness with their fingers while the men hunted rabbits and quail. There were no cities then, only villages where bronzed people lived a simple life.

We could sense the pulses of the Indians who lived here. We could feel a kinship with them. We could wonder who we were and wonder why we were here. We could wonder where we were from and where we were going. We did wonder about these things.

Angela was raised in the city Detroit until her parents moved to California; I in the country, Colorado, Louisiana, parts of Texas. She has seen concrete and nickel and asphalt, huge towers of granite, while I have lived close to the land where rocks and trees and wild things draw a young boy into the mystery of life. She has put on bathing suits and swum in chlorinated pools while I have skinny-dipped in woodland glades where the water moccasins eased in lazy scrawls through the dark waters.

We were conscious of life here, past and present. Life swirled around us everywhere we went. We could see the smog hovering over the dam at the west end of the lake and feel a constriction in our throats. It wouldn't be too long, we knew, before the deadly air began to infect us, this lake, this land.

We are trying to tell you who we were, why we were here. It was more than the air we breathed that made us happy to be here. It was more than the land.

We knew it must finally be ourselves. This is why we came here. We were mountain people by then, and we couldn't explain it beyond that.

We were the Serranos, the miners, the coyotes, the grizzlies who roamed this valley a hundred years ago. We were Atlanteans who came from a catastrophic event that plunged our civilization into the sea. We were many peoples, many countries, many minds and beliefs.

We were seven thousand feet above our past, yet close to it in the way we wanted to live.

We were swimmers out of yesterday who felt oddly at home there, oddly out of place.

Pinewood Lake had become more than a home to us. It had become our destiny.

When the moon drifted behind a cloud, sometimes we could hear drums. We could hear our hearts drumming.

~ Angela's Eyes ~

I could see the death in her eyes way back then.

She had a terrible hangover. Her hair was up in curlers, loose strands sticking out like straw. She was still in her faded blue robe and her feet looked veiny and thrombotic in her tattered slippers. Her eyes were dark, sunk far in their sockets, the circles under them not of the flesh but reflections, taints from her eyes.

She had been drinking for three days and was very thin. Her hands, veiny as her feet, shook and she drank a lot of water, throwing it down as if to quench an inner flame that wouldn't subside. Her skin, where it showed, was yellowish with blue blotches on it. Bruises, I suppose, where she had clutched herself as she lay unconscious in a fetal position.

Colin just ignored her presence.

I stayed out of her way, observing her, though, looking at those terrible eyes and the death inside them.

She wrapped her rolled-up hair in a four-color silk scarf of mine. I hadn't worn it in a long time. The lumpiness and size of her head on top made her face look very narrow and small, emphasized her eyes. She poured herself a glass of milk, fumbled some dry salted crackers from a box, and sat at the cedar table. She nibbled the crackers and drank the milk, stared at the far picture window without seeing anything.

Colin drove his little toy car into my work room where it was cool and quiet and serene.

I lost all interest in the magazine I was reading.

"How do you feel?" I asked finally, because it was so quiet and there was nothing else to say.

"I'm all right." There was a snap of irritation in her reply, faint, but discernible.

"Aren't you sick?"

"Yes, I'm sick!"

I let the hurt and the anger rise up in me. A game to play with no winners.

"You ought to be."

"Just leave me alone."

I got up and walked over to the table. She glared at me, but the anger was for herself as much as it was for my intrusion into her guilt world.

I looked at the death in her eyes and felt my stomach weaken, churn.

It was death all right. But whose? Hers? Mine? Ours? Or just the death of something we once had, or thought we had.

~ *Secrets* ~

Talk began to build about the dead man, Smith, the one who was shot that night Angela and I had walked to the movie. Talk began to build about the woman who had shot him.

In a small town like that, talk was inexpensive.

Other murders were discussed.

Some said Laura Foxworth shot Herman Benson. She was a young blonde built like a Thoroughbred. Herman was a thin man with a scar on his personality.

Others said it was Darlene James who blew Carl Williams to hell. She was thickset and angry, while he was an axe-faced man who fished in summer, drank in winter.

The stories went on and on. No one ever called the sheriff's office to find out who killed them. The bartenders, who are the wisest of all because they hear every tale and embellish every spurious fact oracularly, said the sheriffs didn't know who was killed nor who the killer was.

In the matter of Smith, they were right. I checked.

I told Angela about it, after spending some time in the Kaos, the central bar of town.

"How do you know for sure they don't know?" she asked.

"I don't. But bartenders usually know everything."

"Why?"

"Because they serve the drinks to the guys who come from court, who are on the grapevine."

"They're not really qualified," she said.

"No, but they're weather vanes. They know a lot more than the sheriffs sometimes. Talk in bars is private, but public."

"I don't understand."

"A guy tells a bartender things he wouldn't tell his psychiatrist. These guys can't afford a psychiatrist. The barman is the shrink. Come on, Angela, don't be so naive."

"I thought psychiatrists were out of fashion."

"They are. Bartenders aren't."

"So, who killed whatshisname?"

"I don't know. But somebody here knows. Everyone is tight lipped. Pinewood Lake is like that."

"That's the trouble with this place. Everyone knows everything and no one says anything."

She looked very sad after she said that.

It was true, though. There were few secrets there. The secrets themselves were really open. They shone on a man or a woman like badges. They were buried in the lake, like moonlight, and they surfaced once in a while when you were not prepared for them.

I didn't know anything about the murdered man or the woman who killed him. Maybe it was the nature of the town not to know too much when it would be inconvenient. Small town, people wanting the status quo, etc. Somehow, though, this had become important to me.

I didn't want answers to the killing so much as I wanted answers about the people here who kept such things secret.

I looked out at the lake that night, wondering, hoping for answers.

Angela was at home preparing supper, thinking her own thoughts.

A man came up here once and killed a grizzly bear, I thought. He started it all. Gold, silver, lumber, commerce. Now there were innumerable real estate offices, gas companies, a telephone exchange, construction, hustlers, more killings.

The lake looked very sad, very uncomplaining. Well, it was man-made. It had nothing to do with such things. I glared at it, expecting no answer.

Yet it winked at me like a wise star.

~ *Angela's Nightmares* ~

Angela rose out of sleep like one of Homer's dawns, rosy fingered and tossing. I had been up for hours, writing the things in my head, and I missed her. We had been cheated of each other for all those moments, and I felt guilty. She was very cranky in the mornings, but I had her coffee ready for her.

She pulled out of it after a while. We had made love the night before and she was not obsessed with her crankiness after her mind had settled back into its cradle. It had been roaming around the night, snatching dark dreams out of the cosmos, flying everywhere in her own peculiar form of astral projection.

"I had nightmares," she told me.

"Let's hear about them."

"I can't remember them."

"If you could," I said, "we might find out what they meant."

"They were horrible."

It is difficult to be sage at that hour in the morning. I had kept her huddled next to me all night and she still had the nightmares. She must send her mind away somewhere, I thought, into Hades or into Freud's realms, into the collective unconscious of a million years of human history.

But she had come back and I welcomed her.

I could see that she was badly shaken, however.

I wondered where she had been.

Sometimes, she would remember.

"It was a large room," she would say, "and there were many

people, friends and strangers. I was trying to get to you, but you were far away. There was laughter and people clawing at me. There was an awful presence there.

"We go out on the huge lawn," she said, switching to the present tense, "and you run to a car with a pretty girl. I scream and hear the sound of wings in the dark after you leave. I run into a river, or a lake, and I am soaking wet, screaming. I have things crawling over me. There is no light. I am drunk somewhere, on a street, in a city, then locked up, kept away from you. It's horrible."

It was horrible and I couldn't yet fathom that world of hers.

She was very far away, with strangers she knew in dreams. She was in the lake, struggling to get out. She was racing through the pines all alone, a frightened creature with no home, no friends.

I reached for her in the daylight, when I could see her.

But there was always a shadow across her face, a pain in her eyes, a fleeting look of fear apparent in her visage. Beyond her, there was the lake, shining like some eerie halo around her head.

Suddenly she is a Renaissance painting of some worried woman, a saint, perhaps, who has known much trouble, seen many horrors before seeing light. She seems transfixed there over her coffee, its steam rising up before her like a scrim of gauze, fading away like an old and tragic masterpiece.

I wanted to love her very much, before she faded away completely.

I wanted to love her very much before she drifted into sleep again, before she disappeared into some terrible past that threatened to rush up to the present.

~ Conversation ~

There were some boats on the lake one clear night. They looked like campfires built over mirrors. I watched them for a long time and wished I had a boat of my own.

Angela was sitting in the car with me by the lake.

"It's a nice place to live," I said.

"So pretty."

She was like a doll-mannequin, programmed to speak. I was sure my conversation was full of deeper meanings, but I could have been wrong. The boats were articulate, distant, floating, like half-heard conversations at congested parties.

From one of the boats I heard laughter.

I looked at Angela and wanted her very much.

"I want you," I said.

"It's so pretty out there," she said, programmed.

I held her close and she responded. We kissed.

"Let's go home."

"It's so pretty here."

The boats maneuvered like lighted game pieces on a crystal board. I could see the phalanxes of Roman armies gathering for battle. I could see the plains of Gaul, the bannered legions, the cohorts assembling in even ranks.

One of the boats had a radio blaring.

It destroyed the night, the lake.

"Angela, let's go home, sweetheart."

"If you want."

I moved back to the steering wheel. It's so pretty here, I thought. I'll stay and know we can't be kids again, even by this kid lake. Nineteen forty-nine is gone. Nineteen fifty is gone. The old Ford is rusting with the shadows of necking teenagers floating about its rotted upholstery. The '50 Chevy is sunk in the lake, a skeleton of Sinatra songs and hop dances, wild hands and saucy hamburgers.

The boats shimmered in the footlights, blurred by sudden old tears.

~ *Fishing Again* ~

Angela just sat there on the bank at Sansone's.
She was looking out across the lake, the sun making her dip
her eyelashes. Her eyes were so dark anyway, darker still that way.
I had offered to buy her a fishing license but she said she didn't
want one.

Colin was playing with a line I had rigged for him. It had
only a red-and-white bobber on it. He threw it in the water and
retrieved it. He thought he was fishing, like Daddy.

Nobody ever fished from the bank at Sansone's, except me and
Smiley and a couple of other smart boys, Jake Carter, his wife
Candy, and a fellow called Shorty, sometimes Gideon, a laundry
truck driver who was always late with deliveries.

I almost always caught my limit there. I liked to have Angela
and Colin there because I felt guilty leaving them at home. It was
not good fishing when they were there, though. People who don't
fish are distracting to a fisherman.

I wasn't a good fisherman, but I wanted to be. I had learned a
lot of things from Smiley and from Gideon. They were the two
best fishermen on the lake. They knew all the good holes. It was
still too early to go out in a boat, so we fished at Sansone's or from
the observatory pier.

The observatory was the only thing on the lake that didn't
look right. It was white and the dome turned with the sun all day.
At night it just sat there like a mushroom in the dark, oblivious
to the heavens.

I landed a small rainbow and Angela looked up at me with a smile. I was very happy.

"They'll get bigger," I said.

"Look, Colin," she said. "Daddy caught a fish."

"Fishy," Colin said, and tried to grab it in his tiny hands. I put it on the metal stringer attached to my spike, slipped it back in the water. It swam frantically in circles, trying to escape.

Angela looked back down at the water. Colin started throwing pebbles into the lake, off balance, delighting in the splashes.

"Watch him," I told Angela. "He could drown in a minute if he fell in."

She held on to him, but he didn't like it. All of this made me very nervous. No one likes to think of these things. Colin was very small, though, and would panic if he fell in the water. He would gulp it all in as he tried to breathe. There was no way to teach him the danger while he was so young.

The sun climbed high. I drank three beers. We ate sandwiches. I caught four trout, small ones. Angela smiled at me.

On the way home, Colin fell asleep in the old Chevy pickup I'd bought. I cleaned the fish and stored them in the freezer. They had lost all their beauty by that time. We ate hamburgers and talked a little.

"Why don't you like to fish?" I asked Angela.

"Oh, I don't know," she said. "I just don't feel comfortable."

"But you used to fish with your first husband, didn't you?"

"In the ocean."

"This is just as much fun."

"I will someday," she said, looking far-off again, the way she always did when I got close to something inside her.

"You'll like it," I told her.

"I think I would."

The way she said it, I knew she wouldn't. It wasn't the fishing that she disliked, though. I could tell. It was the water. Every time we went near the lake, she changed. She withdrew. There was something about the lake she didn't like, that made her feel uncomfortable. It wasn't the fishing.

It was something down in the water, something deep inside herself.

~ *Voyeur Moon* ~

One evening we realized how close we were, Angela and I.

A piece of moon came up when we walked outside at dusk to look at the lake. When I looked at Angela, the moon had taken up a corner of her eye, like jewelry, like a frozen tear. She looked very lovely just then. She smiled and I felt my stomach twist with a sudden spasm.

I took her into my arms, kissed her.

The moon fell away as she closed her eyes.

She was warm against me for a long time.

When we got to the lake, we were young lovers, walking hand in hand to an old prom down a country lane. We were school chums dazzled by the star-sprinkled night, caught in a hush of mystery. Angela had never looked so inviting before.

She invited me.

Oh, the moon, the voyeur moon. What a sight it was as we rustled in cloth, trying to divine the mystery. It winked over us with a knowing silver smile, the lewd and kindly moon. We laughed back at it with the arcs of our bodies, while the pines bathed us in a balmy fragrance as though summer was forever, nestling at the lake.

We were very close, just then, Angela and I.

The lake shrank into a cozy lagoon somewhere out in the South Pacific. The pines metempsychosed into palms. From the clean sandy shore we could see the mast of our sailboat tossing from side to side with the motions of Tahitian waves. We could feel the hot sand beneath our bodies, hear the lap of the waves on the beach. We were very primitive, Angela and I.

We were in love.

This was a small love story that starred us both. The marquee proclaimed our endeavors in the shimmering lake while the moon kept smiling.

We were a big hit, Angela and I. There was applause from everywhere all the way home.

~ Out in the Woods ~

I have never lost anything in the woods here.

Once I almost lost my temper, but the wind rose and took away my anger so that I forgot what I was mad about. The wind is that way here. If you're out walking in the woods, thinking over a problem, and you tend to get uptight, well, the wind will come up and wash away everything that's bothering you.

One day when I was miffed about the hurt dealt me by that old grouchy Jack Ennis, president of the Grizzly Prospector's Club, I walked in the woods. He had accosted me at a dance over in Little Deer and publicly accused me of trying to undermine the club. He was wrong and I told him so, but some men don't believe the truth because they don't know what it is.

The woods made me forget his frog face, his lung-burning cigar, his troglodytic manner, his crude speech, his bowed legs that made him swagger like a bully as he walked around wearing a big gun on his hip and fifty badges on his cowboy vest from past Grizzly Prospector's times.

The pines have a way of becoming harps when the wind blows.

Everything in the forest listens. A ripple of needles sounds like plucked strings. Chinese good fortune chimes, a child's comb and paper. I've sat under a tree for hours just listening to this kind of music. My shoulders loosen up as though they were being massaged by invisible fingers. My brain floats on a cushion of mindlessness. This must be part of what transcendental meditation is all about.

Sometimes I would say the word *Ommmm* and feel my lips vibrate mysteriously, my body tune up to the cosmos.

Everything seemed more alive and more at peace at those times. Ants would scurry through rotting, downed timber, harmlessly carrying out their tasks. Birds would flit by as if to welcome me to their haven. Squirrels chattered to me. I felt like St. Francis with my crumbs and goodwill.

I am very small out in the woods, yet very big. It is something I can't fully understand. I am a stranger, a visitor, yet I feel at home. It's as though I had walked into a Goldilocks cabin and found it clean swept and homey, porridge on the table, a bed to nap in when I had taken my fill.

I had never lost anything in the woods there at Pinewood Lake.

I had only found something that is hard to explain.

The woods are a place to dream when you're wide awake, just like a school window you looked out of when you were a kid in spring, your soul barefoot as a Tom Sawyer.

~ Songs of the Wind ~

Songs were coming through the eaves of our chalet.
The wind was up and the pines were tuned to its passing, its violin travels. Some people are terribly disturbed by such music. Angela thrived on it. So do I, still. Colin used to laugh when we asked him to listen to the high travels of the wind through the green forest.

Sometimes in the afternoons, Japan would come to our home. Bamboo chimes in the forest. An ancient sound of ivory chopsticks in wooden bowls. A shuffle of feet on polished hardwood floors, the rustle of silk, quiet smiles in hallowed rooms. Kerouac on a roof in San Francisco, talking quietly with Ferlinghetti as the breeze from the bay sniffed over the multileveled city. Gary Snyder in robes, talking to Phil Whalen; Allen Ginsberg writing Kaddish in an ancient Semitic alphabet.

Sometimes you could feel the arctic chill of the Klondike, deep in your lungs. Once, though, it was Malcom Lowry's lonesome breeze coming down from British Columbia with a taste of fire, a smell of docks pushing into the sea. A zephyr from Big Sur had the bite of Henry Miller before he moved to the Palisades, a taste of sour French wine, a drench of Brooklyn streets.

Angela would move out onto the back porch like a dancer gliding across the stage like a puppet on strings to the music of a symphony orchestra. There was where the air was the sweetest, fullest.

We could see the lake in our minds, jiggling in breezes, all meringue, tossed and frozen in fragments caught in our quick curious eyes. Angela danced in the wind like a song, though she was standing still.

The wind believed her; she believed the wind. And the summer carried many messages in its telekinetic breezes, like song.

~ At the Sheriff's ~

I tried to find out who killed Smith. I went to the sheriff's office. I felt very uneasy. I felt like a criminal myself.

The sheriff's office is down by the lake. The boys like to fish out back when things are slow. There was a young deputy on duty and a lady deputy drinking coffee, talking to him.

"May I help you, sir?" the young deputy asked.

"Yes, I wanted to inquire about that killing last spring. Of a guy named Smith?"

"Smith?"

"I think that was his name."

"What's your interest?" he asked suspiciously.

"Well, I just wanted to know if you caught the murderer or not. I'm a writer."

"Oh, I see." He went back to the desk and whispered to the lady deputy. They giggled. I hated that.

I tapped on the top of the Dutch door, the bottom part that had a ledge. My knees were wobbly.

He came back over.

"Where'd you hear about it?" he asked.

"Over the radio. In the newspaper."

"And you want to know who killed him?"

"Yes, I do. If you caught her?"

The deputy laughed.

"Her?"

"Was it a woman?" I asked.

He laughed again.

"Don't you know?" he asked.

"No, I don't. That's why I'm here."

"Why, that was cleared up a long time ago."

"It was?"

"Yes." He laughed again. "Smith killed himself."

"I don't see the humor there," I said.

"You heard it was a woman suspected, right?"

"Right."

"Do you know why?"

"No."

He leaned over then and started giggling. I waited. It took him a while to straighten up enough to speak.

"We always look for a woman in such cases," the deputy whispered. "It was suicide, though. That was proved."

"I don't get it, Deputy. What's the joke?"

"Well, Smith shot himself in the balls," he said.

~ Independence Day ~

Fireworks are illegal in the mountains. They have a fireworks display on the lake at night every fourth of July, but that's it.

Angela and I went fishing the morning of the fourth with Colin down by Condor Point. We caught a dozen bluegill and ate sandwiches. We were out of the stream of tourist traffic. When we drove home, we were grateful we didn't have to be anywhere or go anywhere.

We drove by the American Legion Hall. The bar was open, of course. We saw lots of cars there. We could tell who was there by the cars: Broncos, campers, Cadillacs, and Lincolns. It seemed like the regular legionnaires were all there. That's their way of being patriotic. They go to their own bar and get drunk. One of the men, I've heard, played "The Star-Spangled Banner" on the jukebox over and over. He saluted the flag every time it played.

We celebrated Independence Day by being independent. We were sober, too.

Hooray for us! Hooray for the people! Hooray for Independence Day!

~ *The Warning* ~

There was something in the air that night.

Pieces of wind that didn't go anywhere. Like cut-off sentences spoken in whispers. Shreds of breezes that waffled into silence when you felt them coming near. Disjointed sounds licking at the eardrum, teasing the mind with little pinpricks of muttered gossip in the subjunctive mood. Fragments of prepositions. Hammered chunks of questions. Half-truths. Beginnings of secrets, tails of insights. Intangibles.

I sat on the back porch steps trying to draw them all together into something coherent. I sucked at them like a man filling his lungs to clear his head. I rubbed my forehead, squeezed my temples, drew my fingers together from opposite points across my closed eyes. I grimaced, twisting my facial muscles as if this would bring knowledge, perspective, point of view. I looked up at the back wall of the house, toward Colin's window. It was dark there, too, and I knew he was asleep. What was I looking for? What did I want to know? To hear?

Angela opened the back door. Some light poured out on the porch, the steps.

"There you are. May I join you?"

"Sure. It's quiet out here." I scooted over on the steps and she sat down. Maybe that was what I needed, what I was looking for. Maybe I was waiting for her all this time in the dark. The moon had not yet risen but I could see the outline of her face from the faint light of the living room. The light had traveled through the kitchen and come to rest on her face. She was pale and lovely as if Vermeer had painted her suddenly. I took her hand.

"Worried?" she asked.

I was surprised. "A little."

"About me?"

"About you. About us."

"What about you? Yourself?"

"I guess so. I don't know what you mean."

She sighed deeply. Like a piece of wind that didn't go anywhere.

"Johnny, I love you," she said, moving her hand over mine and squeezing. "I know I've hurt you. I haven't meant to but that's no excuse, no explanation. I'm in trouble, I know that. But that's why I worry about you. I know you're in trouble because of me."

"We'll work it out, Angela. When you get better . . . when we understand this thing, this disease, this whole nightmare . . ."

"See? You don't know. You can't explain any of it. Neither can I. Don't you want to know why I'm worried about you?"

"There's no reason to worry about me. If you could just worry about yourself, get yourself well."

"No, you're avoiding things, Johnny. I know I'm sick. I know I'm weak. I know I need some things, and some things I can't get. I've seen the bottom. I've been to the bottom. I've been in the pits, in the dark. I've been in hell."

"I know you have, but I don't see what you're getting at. I mean, if you know all this, why do you keep going there? And why would this make you worry about me?"

She took her hand away from mine and put both hands on my face. I could see half of her face very clearly. It was a dull sweet orange. The other half was in shadow. The light source gave her a look of mystery, of feminine power that was impressive. Vermeer again. It made her nose seem very straight, very regal. And her eyes bored into me like arrows.

"Johnny . . . Johnny, it's so hard to say it. You see things so, well, so pure. Or you want to see them pure. Everything. Listen to me. Please. You want everything right. Even your writing you hate because it's not right, it's not what you want. Oh, I don't mean great, just . . . just the best you can do. And that's what worries me. You write about what you want to see, not what you see. Even when you write about villains you make them attractive, give them some . . . some reason for being bastards. You're the only person I know who can write about a garbage can overflowing with filth and make it seem beautiful. You have the right words, you just don't see the ugliness in the garbage can, in life, in me, in yourself. Wait, don't stop me. I've got to get this out. You see, even in my worst moments there are . . . revelations. Insights. Things I can see and know are right.

"I worry about you because you don't see how . . . oh, I don't want to say the wrong word, weak is what I was going to say, but it's not that . . . it's how unprepared you are for the bad things in life. Can't you understand? Can't you see what I'm trying to say? You go blindly around thinking you can save me, that you can help me . . . but you can't. I'm the only one who can help me. No, don't get down on me, don't shake your head. I'm right. You just can't see that you're the one who needs help . . . not from a sickness, but it may be a sickness or something like that, a goodness in you that can go rotten, sour.

"I'm not going to stop, so just listen, Johnny. I'm trying to get it out. Trying to save you. Look at me. I'm trying to tell you what I feel, what I know. You're the kind of man, the kind of person who's going to fall hard. If something bad hits you, you'll just go down. I don't want that to happen to you. You can't just go on writing the kind of stuff that kills you inside and think you're doing a good thing supporting Colin and me. You can't go on martyring yourself and hoping I'll be sober, that I won't take a drink again, that I'll be . . . what? . . . oh, something you want me to be or think I am.

"It's . . . it's hard to put into words. All this. I just . . . just get so mad at myself because I don't have your words. You have them, Johnny, and you waste them on crap. I'm not putting you down for it, I just see the . . . what? . . . the edges in them, the between the lines. You need to be free of my kind of responsibility, my worry, but . . . well, more than that, you need to get down to the bottom of yourself, the hell of yourself . . . it's there . . . something's going to hit you some day and you'll just fall apart. You have no . . . no armor. That's it. You have no protection. You're frail, Johnny. Frailer than I am. Dammit. Can't you see it?"

She fell on me then, weeping.

Those fragments, those pieces of winds and conversations, of sounds and half-truths all picked up momentum. They came funneling down to me in a rush. Too fast for me to understand. Too much for me to absorb.

It was chilly on the steps. Cold. I held Angela against me as she sobbed out her frustrations. I hadn't the least idea what she had been talking about. But she had talked. She had spoken to me. It was all very puzzling, but it was something to add to the things I felt. I loved her. I knew she was getting well. She was coming out of herself, out of her shell.

I felt good about it.

She was sober and she loved me.

There wasn't a thing to worry about.

We went inside and turned off the living room lights. We went upstairs and made love. I felt very strong. Some things made sense. Some things bothered me. But she was wrong. She was merely projecting her own weaknesses onto me. I knew that. She had been talking about herself. She had put her own problems on my shoulders.

I was grateful.

I was the strong one.

Still, I wished I had listened more carefully to her warning.

~ The Country ~

We went to see some country one fine day. Canyons, valleys, things like that. The sun was leading the way, pointing out places of interest with golden thoughtfulness.

Angela and I drove, with friends, over some old washboard roads used by pioneers a hundred years ago. It was a pretty rough trip in the old Jeep owned by Pat Dims, who let me drive it because I was afraid to let him handle it over that kind of country. Pat can't drink very much beer, but he drinks a lot of beer. He loses his judgment after a few.

The country opened up to us, to Pat, his wife, Layne, to me and Angela, like the pages of a Zane Grey western.

There were plateaus and mesas, which may be the same for all I know, and jagged razorback hills, purple mountains far off, and yucca valleys. We even saw a cactus, barrel-shaped and spiny, full of hidden juices we wished we could taste. We saw some topknotted valley quail and plenty of doves moving through the air like erratic darts. Squirrels and chipmunks, lizards and yellow orioles, kept showing off by crossing the road in front of us. It was quite a display of wildlife and I wished I had a way of holding them all in position while I painted them. They were all too fast.

Pat and I drank beer while I drove. We took a lot of side trips, looking out at vistas that broke over the eyes like fresh waters full of sudden flowers. Once, in the distance, I thought I could see some of Louis L'Amour's Sackett clan riding down a trail to help their brethren. I knew I could hear a lot of old ghosts mining in the nearby hills with picks and hammers and jiggling boxes of grit.

One mine was a painting. It was all done in red ocher. It was called the Red Mine. Its hills of tailings had already become small mountain ranges. I could see the earth in miniature. Pat and Angela and Layne all exclaimed about these phenomena. Rain had shaped these reddish hills into spires and parapets. If you blocked out the rest of the world, they looked like a model railroader's domain. You expected a small ore train to come around a hillside any minute.

Later, from a high hill leading to a circular valley, the red tailings looked like Indian burial mounds. I could feel the thrum of the Serrano drums beyond the eerie graves of waste. I could see the arrows fly as the Indians came charging down on our Jeep right out of a western novel, hollering from the pages in rude vengeance.

All day long the history of the new country unrolled before the pounding wheels of our Jeep. We were riding a bronco through storied lands almost a century after they had been condemned through progress. All my notes flew out the window as we hurtled back home.

Back from the glorious West of yesteryear.

~ A Look at the Stars ~

We often went outside to look at the stars before we went to bed. During the winter, we could hear a pack of coyotes bellering up the slope of the mountain. In the summer, though, it was very quiet. We didn't go outside and look up at the night sky anymore. Angela seemed to have lost interest in such things. Her drinking was worse. It wasn't all the time, just once in a while. But it was a dangerous kind of drinking.

She sneaked vodka and pretended that she hadn't had anything to drink. I could tell she was drunk, though. Supper took hours to fix. Then, when it was finally ready, she wouldn't eat. She just sat there and stared at her plate. And she babbled.

She talked about nothing. She repeated the same phrases over and over. I tried to pretend that she was just talking about what was on her mind, but it was no use. I knew she wasn't really saying anything. She was like a schizophrenic. She was talking about things only she could see. She was a desperate woman, and I felt helpless.

I went out and looked at the stars one night. Angela was sitting on the bench at the table, her plate cold, the food just worried about, hardly eaten. Colin came out with me and I showed him the moon. He liked looking at it. He liked pointing at the stars. There was a strong scent of pines, a little breeze working down the slope in our direction. He kept saying, "Moon, moon," over and over. And pointing.

Inside, his mother slumped over the table like a woman hanged, her hair floating over her face, hiding it.

The stars and the moon were cold. I slammed the door on them, took Colin upstairs, and read a book of Bukowski's poetry until my eyes hurt.

It was some kind of hellish summer. The house was empty. The pines breathed through the window when I turned off the light, hoping to sleep.

About midnight, Angela came upstairs, groaning and babbling. She fell on the bed, passed out. The moon shone through the window, limning a drowned woman washed up on the night tide.

Colin called out in his sleep for a bottle, for his lost mother.

It was a long hopeless night, full of unexpressed thoughts, full of shadows. Sleep covered the three of us like a lake, each of us at different levels, each of us alone, floating, floating like the lost children of Atlantis.

~ Late Summer ~

It hurt us to look at the lake in July.

We saw all the people we knew in its waters. We saw ourselves.

Along the edges of the lake, the buildings grew stolid, in stiff reds and grays and purples, irons along the shores. We could not paint them from our fishing boat, we could not articulate the faceless people behind those facades.

We could only drift away from them, put our lines in the water of Pinewood Lake, and bait our hooks for the helpless hungry fishes of silver, catch the trout like our beating hearts, riffle them to shore and death as the lights from holiday houses danced a dazzled path to our fishing shadows.

The moon in the waters, Venus like a horned finger, tickling Mars. A blush in tiny red ripplings, Neptune a shadow. A dance of planets in the minds of our eyes.

It hurt us to see the sky over the lake this special hushed evening. We could not find our voices, our throats out there on the horizon.

All of our ancestors had come down to the lake, traveling from Minnesota and Michigan, and Iowa, over the plains, the Rockies, singing their wagonwheel songs, singing their trail songs of cattle and wheat and corn and campfires along the rivers down to this place of soft silver fires roaming in ribbons across the lake like memories of old emigrant wagon roads.

We saw their faces and their journeys into the lake. Saw our past coming up to us in sadness.

We saw many years and many centuries.

After a while, we saw the lapping waters, held hands, kissed.

It was very peaceful.

The lake was full of deep thoughts that we could not explain.

Waters and fishes and darkness.

The shine of the moon in curved dark shells, shells tugged by the distant moon.

Silences across the lake, coming back to us as we stood there on the shadowed shore, silences in silver ribbons, sinking, sinking.

And in the core of those silences, the susurrant warnings all breathy and hollow. Warnings in a language we did not know, as if we were strangers, intruders in a room where no one knew us, no one knew our names.

But like wraiths, like the apparitions of those loved ones long dead and gone, the whisperers seemed to know our fate.

I can still hear those icy whispers as I write these words.

~ Nightmare ~

The seeds that were planted last spring began to bear fruit. AA wasn't working for Angela. The sheriff had to come and take her back to the alcoholic ward. She was threatening to kill me, Colin, and herself. I couldn't cope with her insanity anymore. I couldn't reach her. I was a failure. The summer was worse than the spring. We seemed to have come out of limbo and be headed down into hell.

Angela was growing away from herself, away from us.

My own drinking was nothing to brag about. I didn't get drunk. I just kept sloshing down the beer, hoping that would take away the knot in the back of my head, at the base of the skull. It didn't work.

Whenever Angela drank—and she became more clever at concealing the times she drank—I could tell. Even if she had only had a swallow, it showed. But I never could tell when she might want to drink or why.

When she got back from the alky ward, she didn't seem angry or paranoid. She didn't write any more about her experiences.

"I didn't have to go down there," she told me. "You just wanted to get rid of me."

"You were dangerous to yourself and to us. I cried when the sheriff took you away."

"Well, you won't do it again. You'll go the next time," she said.

"I hope neither of us has to go, Angela. You just don't understand. When you're like that, you're not yourself."

"I wasn't that drunk."

"No, but you were very sick. I realize they're not helping you down there. But I can't help you either. You have to help yourself."

"I am helping myself," she said. "I'm doing just fine."

It seemed like I was looking straight into a nightmare. I took all the liquor in the house and threw it out. Angela watched me, laughing hysterically.

"Do you think that will do any good?" she said. "If I want to drink, I'll drink."

The nightmare was screaming at me in the middle of the day. I was awake and burning. That afternoon I drove out to the Sticks, a bar in Pine City. I drank beer all afternoon and didn't get drunk. The owner, Bud Karon, just kept filling up the glasses. Art DeLand came in and helped me. He got drunk and wanted to fight. I went home, untouched by the beer, my stomach bloated as the only evidence of my attempt at total debauchery.

Angela was sober, accusing. She had won this encounter. I had lost. I felt as though she wanted me to join her in alcoholism.

That wasn't true. She couldn't help herself. I could help myself, but instead I tried drowning at the Sticks. Bud Karon had a good laugh on me. I was a failure as a town drunk.

I pouted and wouldn't eat supper with Angela. I raved and ranted, calling Angela every foul name I could think of. Maybe I was trying to exorcise myself.

But the nightmare stayed on, darkening into something strangely true and surreal after I went to sleep.

~ The Dry Lake ~

East of Pinewood Lake is a huge alkali basin, a dry lake that once was full of water. I think people tried to live beside it, to plant things. Nothing grew apparently, and there are only empty shells of old cabins dotted here and there around this dry lake bed. The ground is cracked with desiccation. There are no birds there, no tracks of animals.

When Angela and I took Colin for a walk there, it was very quiet. The lake bed looked like a huge flattened church. Its chalky bottom could have been the residue of granite from a great cathedral. The edges of the lake were thick with dry grasses that looked like a tundra if you shut out the rest of the picture. Maybe there had been a church there centuries ago. Maybe the Serrano Indians used the place for mystic religious ceremonies before they were driven off the summer land.

We thought we could see a place where pews once were. These were long brownish striations in the earth that seemed orderly. You could kneel at them with the sky for a ceiling and listen to things: a breeze running high above and surging through the far-off pines, a mountain quail piping on a hillside, a bird whistling an odd phrase over and over somewhere in the woods.

"You used to like to go to church and sing," Angela said to me.

"I know."

"How come we don't join a church up here?"

"That's it. You have to join. I don't want to belong to anything anymore."

"But we could just go," she said.

"No, we couldn't, Angela. There are people at the door who ask you your name. You have to sign a card. People call you up, pester you, ask for contributions. Remember?"

She sighed. I had to quit going to a church because they wanted me to contribute to every little scheme they had. They had a new scheme every two weeks. It wasn't church anymore, it was an octopus with a collection plate in its maw, reaching out everywhere with its tentacles.

"I see," she said.

"There's only one church I would join," I said lightly.

"Really, Johnny? Which?"

"The Cavalry church."

"You mean Calvary, don't you? Calvary Baptist?"

"No, the Cavalry church." I had to suppress the grin forming on my lips.

"Well, what in the world is it?"

"They worship equestrians."

Angela slapped me playfully and I let the grin break out.

We stayed in the lake bed for a long time, walking along the pews like kids balancing on a fence. It was a church you could go into and worship without having someone put a hand on your shoulder and thrust a felt-lined wooden bowl under your nose.

But we had no bitterness in us that day, nor anymore, about such contrasts.

~ Catalogs ~

When we were first married, before we moved to Pinewood Lake, Angela and I used to send for the United Farm Agency and Strout Realty catalogs. We read these from cover to cover, picking out low-cost secret places in favorite country. We dreamed of owning land away from the city. We thought of a small place all our own where we could learn the values of simple country living.

We bought many of these places in our minds. We farmed them like pioneers, geeing and hawing behind Missouri mules pulling ancient plows. We caught fish in our own private ponds and sat on the porch at eventide watching the sun pull the shadows across our acreage, chickens clucking in the yard, hogs grunting out in the pens, baby goats frisking in the thick grasses.

Once we bought a four hundred acre farm in Minnesota. It had a silo, a barn, a farmhouse, seventy-five acres under cultivation, a stream, a pond, a little cabin for the hired hands. It was terribly decrepit and isolated. There was land for cattle to graze, a stand of pines where deer roamed in burnt-leaved fall, and a cornfield where wildfowl settled during the hunting season. It cost only twenty thousand dollars and we had less than a tenth of that to our name. We bought it within ourselves and saw it grow and feed our hungry children, our neighbors, the hands that helped us with the innumerable chores. It was a good life of the mind.

We gathered eggs and plucked chickens, bred our rabbits, and played with horned goats that were like pets. Our dogs roamed free and our cats had kittens up in the hay loft. We ran through grassy summer meadows and listened to breezes trickle over the ponds where we caught bigmouth bass on ugly popping plugs that snaked over the lily pads. We skated on ice in the wintertime and tucked ourselves away at night under thick quilts while the fire crackled in the hearth.

We took our corn to county fairs and canned fruits and made jellies and jams, churned milk from our Guernseys and Holsteins.

It was a damned good life of the mind.

We couldn't afford it. We were not rich enough to be the pioneers we wanted to be. So instead we came to Pinewood Lake, to gain a foothold, to gather our dreams about us like women at a quilting bee.

We gave up looking at the catalogs once we moved to Pinewood Lake. We staked out a small claim in a country we loved. The chalet and the lot were just big enough for us. We were just big enough for what we had. It was a place to grow, away from the city, away from the fantasy of catalogs.

~ Candles ~

The electricity went out at supper. Angela got some candles from the mantelpiece and lit them. Colin was very excited. He kept blowing them out and laughing. We finally gave him his own little candle that he could blow and put it just out of range of his breath. He made the flame flutter, though, and this satisfied him. He kept saying, "Canul, canul."

Colin looked like he was at his first birthday party, so we sang "Happy Birthday" to him. His eyes widened like marbles rolling up to you. Angela, in the candleglow, was waxen and uncertain. I imagined myself to look like Mephistopheles with a thick mustache. It was very comfortable with the candles lit. They went with the rain that was falling outside, complementary.

I was going to do some writing after supper on the Smith Corona. It was electric, however, and useless.

"I wish I had my old Underwood," I told Angela.

"You should have kept it," she answered.

There were a lot of things we should have kept. I was coming back to those things now. In some future spring, we would have a garden. We'd get some chickens and ducks and raise them, eat their eggs for breakfast. I wanted to have a windmill to give me electricity, a greenhouse for winter growing, a root cellar, goats, pigs, and a porch looking out over hundreds of acres of untouched land where cattle could roam free. I wanted to be able to stroll down to my own pond and catch fresh catfish for supper, lean on a post and chew on a weed, hear the corn rattle when it hailed, and pick watermelons at dusk.

We were looking for our own America, just like everybody else. That was not it, yet, but it seemed to be a foothold on something close to our dream.

After Colin went to sleep in my lap, Angela took him upstairs to bed. She and I kept the candles lit and watched the rain splattering against the front window. We didn't need to talk; our thoughts filled the room with company for both of us. We were the only people in the world just then.

We were on a farm way out in the country. There were no highways anywhere, no neighbors for centuries. The bins were full, the stock bedded down for the night. We were looking through Sears, Roebuck catalogs, thinking of getting a team for the old sulky out in the barn, making plans for planting in March.

The candles sputtered out finally, and the dark snuffed out our dreams.

We got the flashlight off the shelf by the door and trudged upstairs to bed, suddenly weary. I thought I heard the lake creak with the weight of the fallen rain as I crawled into bed next to Angela.

Colin cried out in his sleep: "Canul, canul," and then it was quiet.

~ *Angela's Birthday* ~

Colin went to bed, stuffed with chocolate cake and chocolate ice cream.

We had wine with supper. We were mellow, stayed at the table to talk, neither of us wanting to blow out the candle that made our intimate supper something special. A new watch on Angela's wrist caught the light in its silvery band. She had admired it and thanked me, although she seemed reticent to accept the gift. She drank only one glass of wine; a second one, half full, sat in front of her.

She looked at me for a long time, took a small sip of her Burgundy.

"Johnny . . . do you like it up here, still?"

"Of course I do. Don't you?"

"Yes. Except . . . oh, don't you ever feel like the town is . . . too small or something? I don't mean too small, but something about being small. I feel like it's not really good for us to live here. A feeling I can't explain. Small towns can be cruel. The people are set in their ways. They stick together. Don't like outsiders. They're nice, I don't mean that, but not nice either. Only to your face. On the surface. Do you know what I mean? I mean, and I guess the wine is letting me get these feelings out and thanks for sharing this with me, you're so sweet, I've never had a nicer birthday, but the people here seem to be waiting for us to make a mistake or to stumble. It's like we're being circled all the time, by the people and the houses, and the circle keeps getting smaller and the three of us are in the middle . . . oh, I can't explain it, really, but I get scared sometimes, a lot of times. Everyone's so friendly. But I don't know if they're really friendly because I wonder what they're waiting for, why they're out there judging us. I guess I mean judging, but that's not really what I'm trying to say. Just that they all seem secure and content, they have their businesses and their parties and we go in there and buy things and it's like living here and still being a tourist. Maybe that's it, the tourist thing. It's affecting me. I don't feel permanent here. I get the odd feeling that something's going to come along and uproot us and throw us off the hill and everyone up here will just go on about their business with the tourists and nobody will care because we never really belonged in the first place. I guess it's more like a premonition. But not strong enough for that. Uh, but, like that, a little. People waiting for something bad to happen. Maybe not to us, but connected to us in some way. You don't think I'm crazy, do you? I just, I've just, uh, kept these things inside me for so long and I wondered if you ever got these feelings. Do you know what I'm trying to say? Insecure. I feel insecure here. It has something to do with the town. The small town. Or some small town. Somewhere. As if the town doesn't want strangers in it and there's a rug under you and the people are just waiting to pull the rug out from under your feet and never let you know what the town is really like. Maybe it springs from my folks being from a small town before they moved to Detroit, then California. It has to do with my relatives growing up in a small town, marrying, everyone living there all their lives and dying there. Even though my parents moved, came to California. They still read their hometown newspaper and still talk about who's died, who's divorced, who's in the hospital dying of cancer, and go to their reunions and count who's left alive and secretly smirk to themselves about how lucky they are to have survived and who's going to die next."

She stopped for only a second to take a quick swallow of wine. All of this had to come out, I knew.

"And Pinewood Lake is like Griswold, Iowa, or Wahoo, Nebraska, or Pierre, South Dakota, or any of these small towns where the population stays the same as old people die and the young ones stay there and start getting ready to die and everybody old gloats when the kids die in car wrecks and hunting accidents and then they come out to California and all live together in a congested community while some little town like Pinewood Lake starts the whole thing all over again. Johnny, I mean I feel their eyes on me every day and even at night, all of them up here watching every move I make as if they know I'm going to fall down and not get up. You've been so sweet, and you like it here, but it's not the town, only the woods and the lake, not the people, isn't it? Do you really like the people here? Johnny? Do you know them? Do you know what they want from us? Do you think they will ever give us anything?"

She drank the last of her wine and looked right through me. I poured her glass half full again. I couldn't answer any of her questions. I didn't know what she meant and yet I did know what she meant. She had dredged up some things from the mud on the bottom of my brain. They were all tumbling out like assorted objects from the maw of an excavating crane. I tried to catch them, sort them out, find out what they meant.

For once I had nothing to say.

Angela had seen into the heart of the town, had threaded through its circulatory system, and probed to its vitals with the skill of a surgeon.

I had nothing to say. I couldn't even acknowledge the fear that started to squeeze a nerve deep in the center of my thorax, and I felt fingers reaching from that nerve toward my heart.

Happy Birthday, Angela! The half-eaten cake ticked between us like a time bomb.

~ Shelter Bay ~

I had to get out of the house. Angela was really wiped out on vodka. She had started drinking secretly in the afternoon and I couldn't stand to see her destroy herself. I drove around to the north shore of the lake. Colin was safely asleep, worn out from a day of playing with the kittens, learning how to walk.

I drove to a place called Shelter Bay. There's a knoll just west of it with a nice small house and minibarn on it. It used to be owned by a movie star but no one lives there anymore. I walked up there because I wanted to be up high, look at things.

It was a clear night. All the stars were spread out like silver coins in an open purse. I felt pretty rich after I got to the point of the knoll.

The lake was calm, the moon was up, full. It was very bright. Shelter Bay was calm and glistening, full of the sky.

I took out my Beech-Nut and stuck some in my mouth, began chewing. I didn't know what to do about Angela. She was another person when she was like that. Not herself at all. I changed, too. I became violent and I don't like that. I wanted to shake some sense into her, to make her see what she was doing to us. She was punishing herself for something only she knew. She must have been. Nobody drinks when they're happy. We were happy, or should have been. We had everything, I thought: a nice home; a place to live quietly, to fish, to hunt, to enjoy the land; a son to raise.

The lake mesmerized me, after a while.

I saw the heavens backward, and the people on the shore upside down. There were no people, but I could imagine them. After a few minutes of being hypnotized, I could see them. They all swarmed around Angela, their hands outstretched. They wanted something, or they were trying to help. Their faces bobbed underneath the waters like silver balloons, like stars, like the moon, like horned Venus in the western sky, like Mars red-eyed and cold.

I spat my chewed tobacco in the water below and spoiled the nightmare.

It was all meaningless anyway. The lake had no answers. Not to a sane man. It was just a lake.

Yet I could see Angela drowning in its waters. She was deep and dark in its depths. Even the moon couldn't save her. Nor I.

~ Kathy ~

Kathy Marceau turned out to be a disturbing factor in our lives, unfortunately. She became an insidious cancer that invaded Angela's shaky mental condition like a tiny grasping octopus cell. She would come to our home and goad Angela into taking a drink while the poor woman was trying to stay sober.

Kathy knew of my wife's struggle with alcohol and preyed upon her weaknesses with her whispering voice: tentacles moving over Angela's fertile, receptive brain sensors where the dark animal of her alcoholism lurked.

"Come on, Angela," Kathy would say, "one little sip of wine won't hurt you. You're uptight. Johnny's having a good time and you're not."

Inevitably Angela would sneak a sip of wine from Kathy's glass. That was enough to arouse the beast of alcoholism from its brain lair, trigger impulsive drinking behavior that was so destructive to Angela, to our home and marriage.

It took me a while to get on to this brutal tactic of Kathy's. I noticed that every time she and Tommy came over, Angela ended up drunk. Then Angela finally admitted it to me one day and I watched for Kathy's move the next time the Elmos came over.

Sure enough, Kathy was right in there coaxing Angela to drink. I blew up.

"You bitch," I said, "you're about the lowest human being I've ever seen. You know Angela can't drink."

"If she wants a drink, don't blame me!" Kathy shouted. I blazed with a sudden hatred.

"Just get out, both of you," I ordered. Angela was drunk because it didn't take much then to turn her mind to a sodden mush.

Tommy tried to explain but he was too far gone to be effectual. Besides, Kathy led him around like a dog, anyway. He was totally dominated by this small, vicious woman who hated everyone or was jealous of them.

"She's jealous of me," Angela said in one of her rare moments of insights. "She'd like to have you for herself."

"Don't be silly," I said. "I've never felt any attraction for Kathy. Just for her art."

"Yes, and that's what drives her crazy," said Angela.

We all have our own insanity triggers. It takes the right person to pull it. Kathy pulled Angela's trigger. I felt sure that if this nightmare lasted, someone would pull mine.

~ *America Dreaming* ~

America was dreaming one still night.

It was dreaming Walt Whitman and Thomas Wolfe, Patchen and Kerouac, Brautigan and Jack Spicer. It was dreaming Thoreau and Tennessee Williams, Hart Crane and Carson McCullers, Eudora Welty and Ferlinghetti, Allen Ginsberg and Bukowski, Burroughs and William Carlos Williams, a hundred poets in a hundred ways, dreamers in dreams within dreams.

The lake was startled by the onslaught of this night flood. It rippled on the surface and churned in its depths like the beginning of a painting by Max Ernst. The moon arched into its waters, became part of the dream, a silver sliver knifing the broken lapping waters. The Drinking Gourd dipped down and scooped up brackish reveries, spilled them back in, danced away like a road song sung by runaway southern slaves.

Everything flowed together, all the dreams of America, like a freight train running over the lake, hawking the night on silver rails, rattling pots and pans, books and election slogans, speeches and sermons, bourbons and Chicagos, field workers and dust bowls, Model-Ts and jet planes, panhandlers and princes, F. Scott and Zelda, nickelodeons and Keystone Kops, Hemingway and Mickey Mouse, groupies and blue jeans, thalidomide and Shirley Temple, television sets and e.e. cummings, baseball and Indian reservations, Robert Service and 3-D movies, Woody Guthrie and chickens in every pot, Eliot and Stein and Picasso and Toklas and Scott and Hem and dope, grass, flower children, Haight-Ashbury,

Grant, Golden Gate Street, inflation, Watergate, Russia, China, San Bernardino, San Francisco, Washington and whistle stops; Pinewood Lake, nineteen seventy-eight, Amtrak, crack up, down into the repository of dreams and planets, the final resting place of personal buddhas, the gold-filled lake that waits for the next seismographic registration like a new eighteen-year-old voter psyched out on all the bombardment of a million American cities all changed forever, still flowing, still quaking under the onslaught of the many fevers and fists and outcrys.

America was dreaming, too, of Crazy Horse and Chief Joseph, of Geronimo and Red Cloud and the Seminoles, the Iroquois.

America was bleeding its dreams into the lake.

And the lake gave up tears and shouts of exhilaration. The lake boomed with the wind cries of America and its endless people, endless dreams, dreamers, revolutionaries.

The dam held and the people of Pinewood slept on, oblivious to the tumult.

Angela and I stayed up late, getting drunk.

"Next week," I said, "I'm renting a boat and we'll go out on this lake."

"Yes," said Angela, slurring her words as much as I slurred mine. "I've been waiting for you to do that."

"I'm going out on this lake and catch something," I said drunkenly.

"I'm going out with you," said Angela.

America was dreaming Johnny Paul and Angela. America was dreaming Colin, too, and here I was, drunk on the edge of an asylum.

Part Four

~ *The Fall* ~

How well I know what I mean to do
When the long dark autumn evenings come.
—Robert Browning
"By the Fireside"

~ Woman of Dusk ~

She came to me at dusk, like a shadow. Kissing, holding me. She opened to me like some kind of night flower. She was sensuous, a honeysuckle tendril waiting for the hummingbird's sip, all arms and legs, Eve, Cleopatra, a wanton.

Her eyes dipped to me, her face dark against my chest.

"Johnny," she breathed, "I want you, want you."

There were shadows across the pines outside our window. Colin was asleep. The sun had burnished the western sky over the far ridges, left its gold trail in the lake like a sword knifing the ripples in a stream.

She kept opening to me. I was drawn into her like a shadow meeting a shadow. We melded together, two dusk shapes in harmony. Gold along the window ledge, whispers of a lake breeze warming its hands in our room, squirrel chuckling in the high branches of a pine.

"You don't know how much I love," she said, "how much I love you."

"Yes, I do."

"No, you don't."

She opened like a night-blooming flower that lives in dark forests under heavy foliage. I could smell her musk. I blended with her, a diving secret bird that visits these secret places.

"Umm," she said, and I understood.

I had opened her further.

There was dusk about us like scented smoke, sounds of our

breathing, our lazy coupling, our love talk. It was very cozy in the chalet this way with autumn holding its breath just outside.

The sun took its gold away, left behind silence and cool darkness. The moon was not yet up, hiding far away in darkening clouds, salmon pink a moment ago.

"You're very sweet, Johnny," she said, dusk pouring from her mouth, her body somnolent in its slow movement.

"So are you," I said.

It was Angela, my shadow, my reflection on a dusky lake of our own. We were very good together; we were tender with each other.

We were part of the darkness, part of the sweet night.

We were loving with the dusk, the night that covered our naked bodies in the soft dark of itself.

We were very happy. Then.

~ *Boats* ~

Angela did not want me to buy a boat.
She did not want to own one. For some reason. Some days, I
rented them. Days when I wanted to go for the deep trout holes,
leave the constraining shore behind.

But dreams are wishes. And wishes are the substance of all
creation. In the beginning was the word. The thought. The desire.
And Mark said, Saint Mark, in chapter 11, verse 24, "What
things soever ye desire, when ye pray, believe that ye receive them,
and ye shall have them."

I dreamed of a boat.

Every time I rented one, I possessed it. Totally.

Each time I dreamed a boat, I came closer to possessing one.

One day, someone gave me a boat.

Rather, they gave the boat to Smiley Pike. I saw him at the
Kaos one afternoon and he told me about the boat.

"Any motor?" I asked.

"No, but some paddles."

"I'll see if I can get you a motor."

"We'll go halves if you can get one."

Halves. Ownership. Half was better than nothing.

I talked to everyone I knew in Pinewood Lake about motors. I
read Mark 11:24 often. I prayed. I began to believe that I already
had a motor.

It occurred to me, one day, that I had never seen Smiley's boat.

"Hey, Smiley," I said to him on an afternoon when violins and watches were limp on an interminable barren landscape painted by Dalí, "is this a good boat we own? You own?"

"Good enough. Want to go down there to see it? It's at Pine Cove."

The boat bobbed there at the little dock like an orphan. Unpainted, streaked with the green paint of former years, gray wood showing on the gunwales, oars resting amidships like platypusian drumsticks.

"Beautiful," I breathed.

"Yeah."

The channel to the lake was choked with algae, weeds. Shallow.

"Needs a motor, really, for trolling," Smiley said.

"Art DeLand has one for me. No prop. Makes a jet of water."

"Perfect. Especially here. No cotter pins, no worrying over the blamed weeds."

"We have to dig it out of his basement. Won't sell it or give it to us, but we can use it. Deal still hold?"

"Yeah. Let's go."

We found the motor under Art's house, decorated with thick cobwebs. There was a fifty-gallon barrel where we could run it. We loaded the ancient tank with 50-1 gas-oil mixture, yanked the starter cord. The motor roared to life. No propeller blades.

Perfect.

Smiley and I lugged the motor down to the boat, tightened down the cinches, took it down the channel.

"It'll do fine," said Smiley.

I owned a boat. Half of it, anyway.

That part had been easy.

The tough part came when I had to tell Angela.

I should have looked into her eyes more closely when I told her. But a man hiding something looks anywhere but there, into the eyes. Yet I saw the clouds there, even so, sudden clouds that appeared out of nowhere like they do sometimes over the lake. Warning clouds. Dark clouds.

Clouds of portent.

But the boat was mine, all mine, then, and I saw my world expanding.

Christopher Columbus. Chichester. Darwin on the *Beagle*. Slocum on *The Spray* out of Boston.

Dead men all.

Old Chris. Probably died happy, ashore, in his sleep. Chichester made it to land. Slocum and *The Spray* were never seen again.

Behind the clouds in Angela's eyes, Charon, the river Styx shrouded by looming fog.

I should have heard the dogs barking.

I should have looked at the bobbing boat moored to the little dock and seen the river beyond.

Instead I saw only freedom. My freedom.

Mark should have said one more thing when he was writing it all down. "Be careful of what you want. You might get it."

Mark didn't say this, but I will.

Be sure. Be careful.

Charon is waiting. The river Styx is often just around the next bend in the road.

Sometimes, Pinewood Lake drains right into it when the earth tilts a certain way and the mind is lulled into visions of immortality.

I know now what Ernie Kovacs meant when he said, "Actually, the earth is flat. People are falling off all the time."

Good old Ernie. He knew.

~ A Night Muster ~

The moon rode the night fall sky like a bold frosty eye looking down on us. The pines reached out for its glow or stood like sentinels at attention. We were being inspected. I leaned against the tree at ease. It was quiet enough for the forest to be heard in its many whisperings. There was something being said in the ranks of trees being reviewed.

"We are alone here."

"We passed inspection."

"This is the way we like it."

And so on.

The moon was the general looking over his many troops.

I was either an outsider or a soldier of special privilege, bathing in the soft light.

Lorca's moon and mine. Angela was watching television inside the golden-windowed chalet, bathing in a frosty light of her own, blackened by images, by talking shadows.

I go gentle into that good night.

I salute the moon as it passes slowly by.

Inspection over. Introspection just beginning.

Look inside, Johnny, look deep. What do you see?

Angela. Dark and frozen somewhere out of all this, yet strangely inside this strange world here.

The lake flares with a phosphorous glow as the moon pours over its waters. There is a steady strobe flash freezing us all for a moment of eternity.

Jory Sherman

Our images bounce into the cosmos like pictures on a television screen. We curve at 186,000 miles a second to the ends of the universe where no one is watching.

I see the close gray pines of night, nothing of myself.

I am dismissed by the moon, blinked away by vast space.

Good night. Good gentle night.

The wind was blowing "Taps."

~ A Decision ~

"You want to go boating, take a picnic lunch?" I asked Angela. "Today?"

"Sure, why not? It's beautiful out there."

"That boat safe?"

"I think so. It's old, but it doesn't leak. We could just loll around, catch some fish."

Angela brightened like a yellow flower in shadow suddenly caught by the sun.

"What about Colin?" she asked. "I don't know who could watch him."

"Bring him with us. He's never been on a boat before."

Angela darkened as though the sun had passed behind a cloud, leaving her in shadow again.

"I'd be afraid," she said.

"Afraid of what?"

"That something might happen."

"What's going to happen? It's a beautiful day. We're a family. We go together. I'll get a life jacket for him. He'll love it."

She thought about that for a minute.

"Okay," she said, brightening again.

She made sandwiches while I took Colin to the sporting goods store to get him a life jacket. They had one his size. They were expensive, like everything else. I bought some salmon eggs for trout bait, some red worms just in case I bombed out on the trout, and night crawlers for absolute insurance. I didn't want to fail in front of my son. We'd catch some fish for sure.

When we got back, everything was ready. Angela packed the cooler with sandwiches, root beer, and beer. She wasn't drinking anything stronger than cola after her last drunken episode.

Colin was excited. He kept saying, "Boat, boat," over and over again. He had seen them on the lake, but I'd never taken either him or Angela on the boat that somebody gave us half interest in.

It seemed like a good day to be on the lake. There were a few clouds over by the dry lake bed, puffy, white, full. Over the lake, blue skies, sun.

In my heart, a miniature of it all.

~ Picnic on the Lake ~

We launched the boat like a buttercup on the lake.
Colin didn't like his life jacket. He kept untying it. He liked the motor, though, and the water rushing past the hull. He sat in the middle with Angela, who, like myself, sat on a blue cushion life preserver. We motored out through thick weeds into open water. I knew a spot not far away where there were trout and bass and bluegill. I could see the fish in my mind like colored anemones flowering below the surface, openmouthed, waiting.

We anchored in a channel near the main part of the lake. I baited up for trout and dropped the line over. Angela didn't have a fishing license. Colin kept fiddling with his jacket until Angela finally took it off. The lake was calm and the clouds banked in the distance. It was very peaceful.

I didn't get a nibble from a trout, so I told her we should move.

"The observatory's got three deep holes off it. The trout aren't here." I started jerking the rope on the motor to start it. It wasn't in neutral so I had to shift it back.

We started out of the channel into the vast expanse of the lake.

Angela looked apprehensive.

"We're going way over there?" she asked.

"It's not far."

"Johnny, I'm scared," she said. "This boat is so small and old."

"We'll be all right," I assured her.

She put the life jacket back on Colin. He was laughing at the spray hitting him in the face. A light breeze was blowing across the lake. It was slightly choppy, but no whitecaps. Everything looked serene. I headed for the white dome of the observatory. I was watching Colin so much I didn't pay any attention to the sky. He was having the time of his life. We'd hit a small wave and the water would spew over the bow, spraying us all. Colin thought that was great fun. The houses on the shore got smaller until they were a child's fabrication, made of cardboard.

The breeze got stiffer and I looked up. We were making about three or four knots, but not moving very much. We were in the center of the lake, forty-five minutes to an hour from our dock. The clouds had moved over and gotten black. They were lumbering elephant herds coming at us. Whitecaps began to appear on the waves.

"Honey, I'm scared," Angela said.

My throat was tight. The shore looked far away. I was not much of a sailor.

"I'd better head back," I said. "It looks like rain."

"Hurry," she said.

A heavy gust stopped the boat in its tracks. My heart swallowed my mind. I could see the rain steaming the lake several miles off, but the wind was at our bow and crushing us in its invisible grasp. It seemed as if we were standing still in the middle of the lake.

I looked around for other boats, but there were none out where we were. Where was the lake patrol? Where were the water skiers? The trollers? There wasn't a boat near us. I had the throttle on full and we just sat there, churning, as the waves got higher. Angela's face was plastic with fear. Colin began to cry.

She took him in her arms as the wind screamed in fury, the

sky blackened. The boat began to take on water as waves hurtled over the gunwales, soaked us with an eerie chill.

"Stay low in the boat," I shouted as the storm descended upon us in full force.

This wasn't real. This was only a lake, calm and peaceful in the mountains. This wasn't the ocean where things could happen this suddenly. I kept trying to head for shore, but was beaten back by the impetus of the waves grinding and crashing against the bow, then against the hull along my port side.

I tried to wish us back to shore, to safe harbor. Angela and Colin huddled in the bottom of the boat. He was screaming and I wanted to hold him, to tell him I loved him. Instead I was cursing the weather, the boat, the small inadequate motor.

I was cursing myself.

~ The Tragedy ~

I've thought back to that day a thousand times. What could I have done differently? How could I have prevented what happened? There is no answer. It was like when I was trying to wish us back to shore. Futile.

The wind grew stronger, the sky blacker. The boat wallowed in huge troughs, tossed like a fragile pod on high waves. We floundered. The rain hit us and we couldn't see thirty feet in any direction. Angela got hysterical and began to scream. I screamed at her to shut up. Colin tried to run away. He was screaming, too.

"Watch Colin!" I shouted.

He broke loose from her. He had unfastened his life jacket and it hung loosely on his small shoulders.

Angela got up, throwing the boat off balance. I rose up, trying to knock her down. A huge wave hit us. The boat lurched sickeningly sideways. Water struck my mouth and gagged me. I felt strangled. The motor sputtered and died.

Then, in slow motion, I saw everything that happened.

Angela went one way, Colin the other. He was tossed over the side of the boat like a matchstick. I saw all this in wide-eyed horror. My voice was gone. I gagged on the water. My arms reached out for him.

He fell over the side headfirst. Angela didn't see it. She was bent over the opposite side, struggling to stay in the boat.

I bolted for my son. His life jacket was torn from his tiny body. I saw him in the water, looking up at me, amazed, his eyes accusing. Angela fell into me, knocking me off balance. I shoved her down in the boat and reached for Colin. He kept going away, his arms flailing, his little legs kicking. I couldn't reach him. I saw his eyes close, his mouth gulp in water. I screamed, but couldn't hear myself.

"Where's Colin?" I heard Angela shout from the bottom of the boat.

I dove over and swam to him. He was four feet under water. He was black and limp. I lifted him up and struggled back to the boat, trying to hold his mouth out of the waves. We were battered back. It seemed hours before I could push him over the side and crawl up. Angela took him in her arms. She was out of her mind with hysterics. I grabbed him away from her and started pushing on his tummy. I breathed into his mouth. I begged him to breathe, to come alive again. I promised God and everyone I would change my ways. I wept. I gagged on my own pain.

The storm passed and we sat out there numb. I couldn't bring Colin back. He was dead. The sun shone on us as we held his poor broken body, his soulless shell.

"My God, my God," I whispered. "Why did you do this to us? Why did you take our little boy away?"

I held his lifeless body in my arms as we motored slowly back to shore at full speed. We didn't care where we landed. We didn't care about the goddamned boat or anything. Colin was gone. Our Colin. Our life. Gone.

The storm had lasted a half an hour. A lifetime snuffed out like a candle flame. On shore, I looked back and saw a speck of orange bobbing in the middle of the lake. Colin's life jacket.

That's when the real tears came, the beginning of our anguished understanding.

Strangers' houses stood among the trees away from the shore where we stood in numbness. One of the houses was close. We needed help with our terrible burden. The house did not look inviting, but it was there, close.

We carried our dead son up to the house and knocked on the door with feeble fists. Angela collapsed when the door opened. I held out my boy to the man standing there.

"We have all been drowned out there," I said.

~ Coda ~

Angela visits me at least once a week.

She brings me chewing tobacco and farm catalogs. We talk some. I show her some of the things I've made out of leather and out of string. I give these to her to take back home to Pinewood Lake. She tells me that she decorates the chalet with them. I think she'd like me to move back there, but I'm the one who asked for the farm catalogs. I am thinking of moving somewhere else when I get out of here.

I will get out of here. The doctor who is taking care of me says it won't be long now. In fact, last week, when I took him for a walk and told him what I saw out there, he was amazed. He said I'd be out next week.

This is a state hospital. It's not in the mountains. Angela arranged that. It is a long way for her to drive, but she does it— every week.

Some of the others used to come down, too, once in a while.

Once Art DeLand came down to see me at the state hospital. He brought me some books about raising rabbits, but I began to cry when I saw a picture of a little bunny. I thought of Colin and what he had missed. Art never came back again. Nobody, except Angela, has.

I am grateful for her strength. She has been wonderful to me, very understanding. For a long time I drew pictures that were full of dark shapes and moving waters. I thought they were very real. I gave them to her and she looked away after she took them. I don't draw them anymore. They are too realistic.

I told Angela what I thought was wrong. I told my doctor, too. Doctor Booker. Tom Booker. I said I thought people couldn't live in small towns anymore. It was wrong for them. They saw too much of the way things used to be. They reached out for each other and couldn't touch one another. I thought it was sad and I still do even though I'm practically well.

I think Angela might have understood. Especially when I told her what I thought about our own situation. She said she had wondered how we had gotten that way and why we had never said the right things to each other. I saw it all very simply after, well, after what happened. The tragedy.

You see, there was this part of me that was trying to see everything clearly. I wanted to see into Angela and into Colin. I wanted to see inside myself. I tried to get into Angela's world and I only got sick. Sicker every time I tried. I got some of her illness, but there was no blame on her part. It was a natural part of the process of our lives in Pinewood Lake. Her illness was really mine and I couldn't see that. I blamed her for being sick when it wasn't her fault at all. I missed something very important there.

I tried to give Angela things she couldn't see, couldn't feel. I didn't feel what she was giving me. I tried, but I failed. All the way down the line. I wanted to love her, but I was on a different path. Born and raised under different stars, I guess. But I don't want to get metaphysical about any of this.

Like with Colin. I couldn't get into his world. I could sympathize with it. I was reaching out for him. As I was for Angela. But, as I explained to Angela and to Tom Booker, we all were reaching out. Colin didn't need me. He had me, but I didn't know it. He was reaching out for his mother. Even at the end, he was.

I was reaching out for both of them, but that was my failure.

I should have let them come to me when they wanted to, on their own terms. I should not have clouded them up with my own visions. I could not impress my genes on theirs. Colin had enough of my imprint so that he was infected as much as I by our life up there. It may have been too much for him to bear. His capacity may have been too limited to handle our troubles.

But all this is speculation. Tom Booker thinks I may have something, though. I told him that I probably cracked because I was the only one who didn't understand and who tried to react without any understanding of life. I wonder about his explanation, but I don't question it very often now. My breakdown was slow.

I was all right during the funeral and with the relatives who came up. I was very strong, the head of the family. After it was all over, Angela and I had a long talk. That's what did it to me, I think.

She told me something she had never told me before. I wish she had told me this before Colin was taken away. We were sitting by the lake one night. We had walked down there, alone, as we used to, trying to get back to normal.

"Did you know how my husband died?" she asked. She had been sober, then, for a long time.

"He died in a parachuting accident," I said.

She paused and looked at me.

"That's only partially true," she said.

I looked at her.

"What do you mean?" I asked.

"His—his parachute didn't open. It collapsed or something. That's what they told me. But they were flying near a lake down south, Lake Elsinore."

I felt the hackles rise on the back of my neck.

"He fell in the lake," she said. "He got tangled up in his chute."

"The fall didn't kill him?"

"I—I don't know," she said. "The coroner said he drowned."

Her husband had drowned. That crushed me. I guess I just cracked up after that. I don't remember clearly what happened. There were days and nights of half-aliveness, fantasy, attempts at drowning myself—in booze and in Pinewood Lake.

Dr. Booker told me a curious thing that I've not assimilated yet.

"Part of your trouble, Johnny," he said, "stems from your being a writer. Especially an unfulfilled writer."

"I don't see how what I do—"

"You work out of your subconscious too much. You're too close to some primary sources that you can't handle. You're like Adam eating forbidden fruit from the tree of knowledge. You gobble it down and don't know what it is. It could be loaded with psychotropic drugs or poison or insanity. You just keep eating and your system breaks down."

"That's a mouthful," I said, "no pun intended."

"Don't worry about it now. I just want you to think about it now and then. You probably won't ever be able to write down everything you feel about your experiences in Pinewood Lake. And what you write down may not even come close to what you felt, to your emotions at the time of your wife's breakdown and your own. Still, if you're a writer, or going to be one, you'll have to try to get at it. Just be careful of how much you dredge up out of your subconscious. Everything's down there, you know. Everything that ever happened to you."

"I know. Maybe everything's down there that ever happened to anyone."

"Maybe."

When Tom Booker and I took that walk the other day, I tried to explain to him how I felt about the mountains, about small towns. I told him how I smelled them, how I felt them go through me like a song. I said that people couldn't touch in small towns. They were too used to the coldness of big cities. In cities, though, people drew together for protection and they developed tough shells. Or they cracked, all right, but they cracked because they were basically loners like me. A loner will crack every time. You have to touch people and if you don't, you crack. He disagreed with my diagnosis of the small town syndrome. He said maybe Pinewood Lake was just my Waterloo. It could have happened anywhere. He said maybe I had moved there to keep from cracking sooner.

I think he might be right there.

Anyway, I cracked.

So they brought me here. Angela was very understanding, as I say. She is a very beautiful woman and I love her. I was just frightened all the time. The doctors now say it was a phobia. Unreasonable. I don't know. I think it was reasonable as hell.

I was afraid of drowning.

But I drowned anyway.

We get what we want, all right, but we get what we fear, too. I learned that much. And something else, too.

Don't be afraid. Of anything.

Ever.